The Dance Hall at Spring Hill

The Dance Hall at Spring Hill

STORIES BY

Duke Klassen

MINNESOTA VOICES PROJECT NUMBER 75

NEW RIVERS PRESS

MINNEAPOLIS · 1996

Library of Congress Catalog Card Number 96-067820
ISBN 0-89823-169-8

Edited by Gary Eller
Editorial Assistance: Carol Rutz
Book design: Will Powers
Book production: Peregrine Graphics Services
Cover artwork: "Cafe Musician," Jody dePew McLeane, pastel on paper, 1995

New Rivers Press is a non-profit literary press dedicated to publishing the very best emerging writers in our region, nation, and world.

The publication of *The Dance Hall at Spring Hill* has been made possible by generous grants from the Jerome Foundation, the Metropolitan Regional Arts Council (from an appropriation by the Minnesota Legislature), the National Endowment for the Arts, the North Dakota Council on the Arts, the South Dakota Arts Council, Target Stores, Dayton's and Mervyn's by the Dayton Hudson Foundation, and the James R. Thorpe Foundation.

Additional support has been provided by the Elmer L. and Eleanor J. Anderson Foundation, the Beim Foundation, General Mills Foundation, Liberty State Bank, the McKnight Foundation, the Minnesota State Arts Board (through an appropriation by the Minnesota Legislature), the Star Tribune/ Cowles Media Company, the Tennant Company Foundation, and the contributing members of New Rivers Press. New Rivers is a member agency of United Arts.

The Dance Hall at Spring Hill has been manufactured in the United States of America for New Rivers Press, 420 North 5th Street, Minneapolis, MN 55401. First Edition.

For LaDes Glanzer

Light of my life

Acknowledgments

"Infinity" was published in a slightly different form by *sub-Terrain* in Vancouver, British Columbia, Canada. "Rimpel-Zimpel" appeared in *Fine Print* in Winter Park, Florida.

Many thanks to my editor Gary Eller of Ames, Iowa, for his dedication, encouragement, and the broad vision that characterized his approach to my work.

I wish to express my gratitude for the encouragement of many friends and readers, including Vivian Balfour, Kathy Carlson, Jeanne Farrar, Jim Goralski, Jay Hornbacher, Kathy Lewis, Jane Lund, Rob Ramer, Pat Rhoades, Danielle Sosin, Alberta Tolbert, Lois Welshons, and Tom West of Athens, Ohio—fine writers all.

I would also like to thank my teachers and mentors at that marvelous Place for Writing and Literature: The Loft. The list includes Kathleen Coskran, David Mura, J. P. White and Myrna Kostash of Edmonton, Alberta, Canada.

I especially want to thank Pat Weaver Francisco, writing teacher *non pareil,* without whose encouragement and insight into the process of writing, this book would not have been written.

Contents

Summer of '36

"Josef. Josef! Where are you? Get in here, you little *Hanswurst.* I'm dying. Damnit, Josef, I'm dying right now." Grandpa Dietrich always wanted something now. He hadn't always been so bossy. I ran into the bedroom, puffing, as if I'd come a long way. He lay in his bed, his pillow soaked with sweat, 385 pounds sagging to the center of the mattress. His body was barely covered by the edges of the sheet. Two butter-yellow rectangles of light glowed behind the shades. Strips of old sheets jammed into the cracks didn't keep out the dust. It was Friday, August 14, in the fourth year of the drought.

"Where the hell were you, Josef? That fan, turn it to the left. No, no! *Wie alt bista doch?* Don't know your own left from your right? When I was your age I had my own plow and team. My brother Payter, too. And Anton. We broke this prairie, grass high as your head, land never touched by a plow, the spring of '65. During the Indian uprising. Who could ever forget it?" He sighed.

Not the Indian uprising again. Everybody knew he was born *after* the uprising. The fan at my back loosened the shirt stuck to my spine. I was in the little spot where Grandpa couldn't see me without cricking his neck.

"Come here when I'm talking to you. *Verdammte Hitz'!*"

My reflection moved in the glass of the Sacred Heart picture but he didn't see it. The bed creaked dangerously as he turned.

"*Ja,* there you are, Josef. Where the hell were you? Get me some ice water . . . if there's any left. You'd think there'd be ice for me." He mumbled, "That woman." He pushed himself up on his elbows. "Wait, if Grandma's in the garden, bring me a bottle of beer. Quick, before she comes back."

"Grandpa, she said no more beer. I'll get in trouble."

"*Bring' es doch, du kleiner Schisser.* Get it, you little shit. I'm not in jail here."

Through the window I could see Grandma carrying water in the pickle patch, the only green as far as I could see.

I ran down the steps into the quiet cool of the cellar and pulled the light. The walls glowed with a hundred reflections of the single bulb, jars of plum jelly, canned beef, corn and peas. I walked through the sweet smell of onions and the rot of last year's potatoes to the stacks of beer cases that Meinulph had brought out from the saloon. Grandpa had counted them, sucking in his breath at each number. When Prohibition came back, he was going to be ready. I opened the bottle and hid the bottle-cap in my pocket. Grandpa grabbed it from my hand. He tilted it to his lips and the beer foamed and ran into the folds of his neck.

"You shake it when you came up?" he asked. I made for the door. "Wait, it's OK. Stay here, Josef. *Danke.* You can run the empty back in a few minutes. Can you move the fan, please? Point it right at me?" He whispered, "Bring me another one, Josef. *Schnell.* Give you a nickel if you do." He gave me his best smile.

"Grandma says not to. She'll kill me if she finds out."

"Everybody's gotta die sometime. It's right there in the Bible—seventy years. I've got that and nine more. I'm not afraid of dying."

He closed his eyes. "This damn heat. Purgatory couldn't be much worse." He peered at me from lowered lids. "I'm having your mother call in the priest. Now don't tell your Grandma." He handed me the empty bottle. "Go. Right now. Bring two." His loud whisper followed me out of the room. *Nein, drei. Drei, Josef. Bring' doch drei.*"

I raced down the stairs, thinking about why Grandma and Grandpa hated each other. I'd heard Mom and Dad talking about Grandpa and the hired girls who had to be sent away. Back when he was skinny. The floor felt cold to my bare feet. I grabbed three bottles, then thought, how old do you have to be to do what you want? I pulled out a fourth and ran up the stairs. The rippled edges of the bottle-caps bit into my fingers.

"You open them," I said. "I don't want to."

He cranked his body against the creaking headboard. The smile that lit his face pushed his cheeks up and nearly closed his eyes. "Bless you,

Josef. You'll go to heaven for this." He pulled an opener from under the sheet. I just stared at the picture of the Crown of Thorns flaming around the Sacred Heart. He tilted his head back, emptied the bottle, and wiped his mouth with the edge of the sheet.

"Josef, *mein Bubchen*, there's a dime for you, right next to my snuff box. That's right, take it. It's yours. Go now. Don't worry, I'll get rid of the bottles." His heavy hand weighed down my shoulder. "Josef, I wish I could still sleep out under the trees with the rest of you. It might make me feel young again."

The next morning the sun woke us from our sleep under the trees. The sheets on our straw beds were covered with dust. Half of South Dakota must have blown over in the night. They said it was drifted like snow further west. Cattle were being driven north to get them out of the heat. Sheriffs were foreclosing on farms all over the state.

After breakfast, Mom and I walked across the road to Grandma's house to help can pickles. I sat on her steps and picked at where my heels were cracked and dry from the heat. They looked ready to bleed. Grandpa's yellow dog, Mips, came out from under the porch. I could hear Mom's voice. "Yes, I'll send Karl over. Maybe an hour. He'll be done with chores by then. He'll tell Jerome and Willem. I'll call Alvina. Somebody will have to go over and tell Aunt Suzanna. Too bad Magnus won't have a phone."

Mom came out and sat on the steps with me. "Josef," she said, "I have some sad news. Your Grandpa died in the night. That's right, Josef. I'm going home to tell your dad."

As we walked home, the gravel burned my bare feet. The dust hung over us. I cleared my throat. "What did he die of, Mom?"

"It's hard to say. Grandma said he looked bad yesterday when she came in from the garden. Maybe it was the heat. It's been so hard on his heart. How did he look to you when you left?"

"He looked like he always looked. Jeez, how should I know?"

"I'm just asking, Josef. Don't be so touchy. And don't say Jeez. It sounds bad." We walked in silence, only the sound of gravel crunching under our feet. "I'm sorry," she said, "you've just spent a lot of time with him, haven't you?"

"Mom, could beer kill a person, I mean, a lot of beer?

"Your Grandpa used to drink a lot but not lately."

I watched her walk to the barn to tell Dad the news. She seemed so brave and beautiful my throat ached. I wondered how Dad would take it. And if he'd ever find out about the beer I'd taken Grandpa. She came back in a few minutes, frowning. "Men," is all she said.

As Dad and I walked across the road to Grandpa's place, the heat seemed to be coming up out of the ground. Jerome, Willem, and Grandma were standing under the popple tree: Uncle Willem, tall and dark, wearing an under-shirt with a streak of dampness that ran down into his pants, Uncle Jerome, shorter and fat like Grandpa, in bib overalls and a long-sleeved flannel shirt buttoned to the top. His face was red. His straw hat was good as new, just a layer of dust in the crown of it. I'd never seen him sweat.

Uncle Willem turned. "Come here, Karl. Talk some sense to Mama."

"Nein," she said, and the cords in her neck tightened. "He's not going to the funeral home. No."

Willem shook his head. "But what about the funeral? We can't have it tomorrow, it's the Feast of the Assumption. Can't have a funeral Mass on a Holy Day. And we can't do it Sunday. Monday's the earliest. We have to take him to the funeral home, Mama. He'll never last in this weather."

"You listen to me. He's not going to the funeral home. Spend good money on a dead body?" Her voice quavered, "We'll have the *Tote'wache* right here. We can handle the wake ourselves."

Jerome's red face shone but he said nothing. Dad looked at Willem. "I don't like it, Willem. What do we do, just go to town and buy a coffin?" Willem's face turned glum and Dad spoke again. "Willem, you're not going to leave it all up to me like you always do. Why should I have to do everything?"

They were still talking when I walked into the house. I pushed open the bedroom door. Grandpa's big white feet were sticking out of the sheet that was pulled up over his face. I looked for the bottles. I opened the closet door: the smell of mothballs. There they were, under the bed. Three of them, anyway. The voices outside came closer. I grabbed the three and raced for the cellar, my feet slipping on the painted steps. I slid them into a case and climbed back up, fast, like I hadn't just killed my own Grandpa.

Dad followed my uncles through the narrow door into the bedroom. Grandma had left for Alvina's. My hand followed Dad's into the holy water font Grandma kept by the door. We crossed ourselves with the warm water and stood next to the bed. Jerome's lips were moving real fast but no sounds came out. Their hands rolled and unrolled the brims of their hats.

Dad's voice trembled as he spoke, "Jerome, you go talk to Father Reiter. Tell him what Mama wants. Find out if he's coming out for Last Rites—maybe close'll count for something. Willem, get over to Davis's and get the biggest coffin they got. Tell him we'll settle up with him Tuesday. And bring along three or four blocks of ice."

. . . seven, eight nine, ten . . . the sky was gray with dust. I was sitting on the gritty porch steps when the *Todes-Glock* started in town. I could almost hear Cletus, the church janitor, stuttering the numbers under his breath. One for each year. . . . t-twenty-six, t-twenty-seven . . . Anybody working outside for miles around was counting with me. They were disappointed when Cletus got into the fifties—no surprises. Must have been somebody old. Who'd been been sick? . . . sixty-eight, s-sixty-nine, seventy, seventy-eight, seventy-nine. Seventy-nine. They were figuring it out. It wasn't Payter. He was sixty-seven. Anton was already dead. It had to be Grandpa or old man Kalter. They'd find out for sure when they came to town with the milk.

The dusty metal coffin had heated up coming back from town. Five fingerprints sizzled where my hand had been. I jumped off the running board and ran around the truck to slip my hand inside a wet gunny sack of ice. Dad and Grandma came out of the house. Grandma stood behind the coffin and cleared the dust from her throat. "It's not wide enough, Willem. He'll never fit in that."

Willem pulled at the front of his shirt, "I had Davis call a bunch of places. It'll be four days before Werner could bring a bigger one up from the Cities."

"Christ Almighty! Four days?" my Dad swore.

Grandma winced. "You needn't curse about it, Karl. You built a barn, can a coffin be much harder? It doesn't have to be fancy."

"You mean make it ourselves? Build a coffin?" he asked.

"It only has to last through the funeral." Grandma said.

"Through the funeral?" Dad's voice rose. "You know, Mama, you're not taking this real hard." Grandma glared back. "Well, it wasn't unexpected, was it, Karl?" Her hand dropped the hem of her apron and she looked away. "A tree falls on you, a baby won't come out, you drink too much, you're dead."

Dad stared. "Forty-eight years of marriage . . ."

"Stop it, Karl. I don't want to talk about him."

Dad looked past the top of her grey head, "God, you're hopeless. He's dead, Mama. What more do you want?"

"Let's get on with it, Karl. That stack of rough-sawn cedar in the machine shed . . . run it over to the lumberyard and have it planed, sand it if you're feeling fancy. You be in charge. Willem, get that metal box out of here."

Dad was in Grandpa's car shed. He sat down, he got up, he walked back and forth, he stared at the pile of cedar. Willem sat on the blacksmithing stump and leaned back against the high anvil. He slapped a yardstick against the side of his leg. A cloud of dust flew up.

Dad stared at him. "I tell you, Willem, it's not easier than building a barn. It has to be light enough to move with him in it. The sides have to be strong enough to attach handles to . . . can't expect six men to pick up a four-hundred-pound man inside a hundred-pound box without a handhold." He hunched his shoulders and watched the yardstick slapping against the side of Willem's leg. "I'm over my head here, Willem. I don't know if I can do it."

Uncle Willem shook his head. "Just get some two by fours, make a frame, cover the sides, make a top, and . . . Bang, you're done. Why you making such a big fuss about this, Karl?"

"Jesus, Willem. You and Mama. You just want to throw him in a hole. He'll lie in it for the rest of time, for Christ's sake."

"So what's he know, he's gone."

"Where the hell did you grow up?" Dad looked up from the lumber. "Besides, it's gotta go to the church. I don't want to kneel there with everybody in the parish looking at how the corners of the coffin don't meet. It's gotta look right. People are used to regular coffins now." He walked over and looked out of the door, then turned. "He's going to be lying in it forever, can you even imagine that? I couldn't stand knowing there's a crooked cut or a gap somewhere, even a nailsplit, you know how cedar is. I can't do it. I could just hear him bitch about it for all eternity."

"Well, damn it, Karl, I said I'd help."

"Right, Willem, you'll hand me the yardstick, stand around and jaw, scratch your head, ruin a few boards, wreck my drill bits and take credit for what I've done—while I take the blame for your part."

"Just one damn minute, Karl. You want help on this or not? You're the one wasted yesterday . . ."

". . . Look, I don't need your help. I take care of my own work . . . and anyone else's who can't pull his own load around here."

"What do you mean by that, Karl?"

"Just what I said, Willem. Pa expected me to drop everything and pitch in for all of you, until . . ."

I was hunched up in the space below the grinding wheel. I couldn't stand that word: eternity. I had this picture of Sister Mary Benedict holding a pointer to the blackboard where she'd drawn a mountain range and a tiny bird, the size of a lilac wren. She sounded angry, her teeth grinding as if her mouth were full of dust. ". . . and every million years this little bird,"—she tapped it twice—"comes back and picks up a single grain of sand and takes it away. . . every million years. You're on your knees in glowing coals, surrounded by your sins, flames licking at your face and hands . . . there's no water. Another million years, another grain of sand. When that whole mountain is gone, then the next mountain, and the next, until that whole mountain range is gone, then—children," she lowered her voice to a whisper, *"Eternity—has—just—begun."* The flat lenses of her glasses caught the light and the reflection made her eyes disappear. She moved her head and they were back, then they were gone again. Just like Grandpa.

"Josef, what's wrong? Why are you crying like that?" Dad bent down and faced me. "Don't you mind your Uncle Willem, he's always been a blowhard."

I was thinking about Grandpa down in the ground and those stories about when they moved our town of Spring Hill from over by the highway, near that bunch of evergreens. When they moved the cemetery, a couple of coffins broke and the tops were all gouged and scratched up . . . from the inside! I tried to imagine that—waking up and wondering if your eyes are working because it so dark and . . . cool . . . that's as far as I could think.

Dad drew the outline of the coffin on a scrap of wood. His pencil stopped. His shoulders drooped and went as round as if he were carrying a side of beef. "We gotta go measure him. I don't know how big to make it."

The door was shut and there was no one home but Grandpa. Grandma was at Aunt Alvina's again. We walked into the bedroom. I didn't want to go in. Grandpa wasn't doing so good in there. Dad turned on the fan and got out his folded wooden ruler. He pulled back the sheet. Dad's face went white, like March. Grandpa looked peaceful but a lot, lot bigger—fatter I guess. "Five-foot-eleven and a half. He's not even six foot tall." Dad's voice sounded like his collar was too tight.

He stood at the foot of the bed with his measuring stick out in front of him and squinted. He held it straight up, almost touching Grandpa, as if he were measuring a snow bank. I stood in the spot where Grandpa couldn't see me. Flies buzzed on the dusty screen behind me. Dad looked over at them, then at Grandpa, then turned on his heel and almost ran for the door.

That night I dreamed about the sheriff coming to foreclose on our farm, and then the sheriff became Grandpa lying in his bed. He became the sheriff again and wanted to lock me up for killing Grandpa. I couldn't help thinking about what had happened to Grandpa . . . what had happend to his soul. Had he counted on confessing his sins before he died? A last-minute confession could save you from hell. I prayed he'd gotten Purgatory. How could God send somebody to hell forever—or to heaven—because of a last-minute confession? It didn't seem fair.

Mom was doing the milking so Dad could finish the coffin. Her blouse had come out of her skirt as she leaned into the cow's hot flanks. She wasn't wearing any stockings. She was a fast milker, even though her arms were smooth and slim; not all muscle like most women's arms. The milk rang out in the empty pail then turned puddlier and more liquidy as the foam billowed up to muffle each squirt. "I talked to Grandma at Alvina's," she said over her shoulder. "We have to figure out what to do, get some more ice or something." She brushed a stray lock of hair from her eyes. "Why don't you help your father? He must have something a big boy like you can do." She always said big boy, when what she was thinking was little.

Dad was not coming to the wake. He had cut the boards and was starting the floor of the coffin. He had borrowed a miter box, some finish nails and sandpaper from Jerome. I walked past the driveway full of cars and wagons. Horses stamped at the flies, round puffs of dust rising from their hooves.

As I walked to the front door, a voice drifted through the screen: ". . . *ja*, they had to cover him with ice; he's rising like a bread pan full of dough. *Ja*, really. I was by the door and I could smell mothballs." I didn't want to hear any more.

On Sunday afternoon, the sun shone through the shed door onto the coffin, which was perched up on the sawhorses. It was finished. Each corner was mitered, smoothed with a rasp, then sanded to match the smooth sideboards. Sturdy handles were cut from two by fours and bolted in place with a polished opening for the hand. The bolts were recessed and plugged with pegs. I could almost lift one end. The cedar shavings smelled like heaven. Dad wanted to varnish it to seal the spaces between the boards. Even Jerome spoke up against that: the dust would stick to the varnish. Dad glanced at Jerome. "It's getting late. Go get your shiftless brother. Let's get this over with."

We all gathered in the kitchen. The coffin stood outside. Willem's voice climbed to the ceiling. "For Chrissakes, Karl! You mean you didn't measure the door? It won't fit through here?" Dad whirled around but Jerome was already there between them. Dad plowed into both of them. Grandma jumped back as a chair clattered toward the stove.

"Stop it, boys, right now." Her voice cracked. "Isn't it bad enough?" She was crying. Jerome separated them but Dad's fists were still clenched. "One word, just one more word, Willem, and you'll be sorry, do you understand that? Willem?" Dad's voice came from his belly. Willem crouched on one knee.

Jerome blurted out, "I . . . I'll get that piece of canvas off the corn planter. We can put Pa in that, carry him through the kitchen. We'll leave the coffin outside." He disappeared through the door.

Grandma sounded mad. "Get up, Willem. Both of you *shtoffels*, come with me." She opened the door and the smell of death rolled out. "Raise those shades, get those windows open. Too late to worry about the dust." She glared back at the door. "Willem, this isn't the time to hang back. Get in here." He didn't move. She turned to face him. "NOW."

Nobody wanted to breathe the air. Jerome schnappered through his nose, as if he'd been running. He handed one end of the canvas to Grandma. "Thank you, Jerome. Take that corner of the canvas and tuck it right next to him." Uncle Willem stood as far away as he could. "For God's sake, help him, Willem." They tried to put the canvas under Grandpa. Grandma stamped her foot and cried out. "It won't work! We won't be able to lift him. Now what are we going to do, Karl?"

"I have an idea," I said. "Put the canvas on the floor, and pull off the end of the bed and slide him down on it."

Grandma squeezed my shoulder. "Good idea, Josef. I'm glad you're here." Willem and Jerome knelt and held up the sideboards of the bed with their knees as Dad and I pulled off the low end of the bed. The smell was even worse near the floor. The stench burned my eyes. Dad whispered, "Easy now, Jerome, let's ease him down." Tilted that way, Grandpa looked like he was on display in a store window. I moved over by the fan where the air was fresher. A brown beer bottle slid out of the sheet and bounced on the floor at Dad's feet. Grandma looked over at me.

Dad put the bottle on the gritty window sill and hid a sly smile. "All right, take the bottom sheet too. Willem, you take his feet, ease him forward." Nobody was looking at Grandpa now, just looking at their hands, guarding their eyes. Everyone's mouth was shut. Willem's top lip was curled back. Jerome's top button was open and his face shone with beads of sweat. I made for the door.

"Wait, Josef, you stay here. We'll need you." Grandma said.

"Sometimes you have to be brave. You and I'll take one corner." My knees went rubbery. We slid him toward the narrow door and I saw he'd never fit.

"We got no choice, Mama." Dad's voice was low. "He won't fit through the door. It's just too damn narrow. The north window is the same size as the door, the west windows are even narrower. We're going to have to take out the two west windows, put a header over them and knock out the post between them."

Willem glanced up. "Right, so how we going to lift him through a window? It was hard enough sliding him toward the door."

Jerome's mouth started to quiver and then opened, "We could make a sling of the canvas, pick up the four corners and wrap them around a couple of two by fours . . ."

"You mean, carry him like a buck out of the woods?" Dad asked. Willem said, "Sure, we could put the coffin in the truck bed right below the window and drop him right in. Otherwise we'll have to lift him. Let's get the bed away from the window and build a step of some kind, then cinch the canvas up tight around the two by fours."

Dad looked skeptical but nodded, "All right, Willem, you start on your step. Jerome, you and Josef knock out space for a header above the windows. There's a pinchbar and chisels in the car shed. I'll get my tools and some lumber." Grandma said nothing.

The sun had set but it was still hot. The wild mint Jerome and I had wadded in our noses helped, but it was hard to breathe. "*Verdammt nochamal.* God-DAMN-it-to-hell. GOD-DAMN-IT-TO-HELL." Dad cursed the nails in the center post and flailed at the final splinter with his hammer until part of the bedroom wall fell away. His eyes bugged out and his neck knotted up. The sweat from his forehead drew little furrows in the dust on his face. Willem came back with the two-by-fours. It would take the four of us to get the sling cinched up around the pole. Grandma was lining the coffin with soft cloth, trying not to hear.

"Careful now, keep him level. We'll boost the pole up to our shoulders. Just take your time. Easy." The heavy bundle of Grandpa swayed as Jerome led the way. Dad and Willem staggered to keep out of each other's way. Jerome was as strong as both of them together. "OK, Willem," Dad said, "I've got it, you run around and help Jerome in the truck." Grandma was sitting on a chair out by the dry well. She looked at me as I came up to her. She wiped the tears from my eyes. The salt from her tears had left white tracks on her papery skin. We looked back at the gaping hole in the side of the house. "Hug me, Josef, I've forgotten what it feels like to be touched." I stood there and hugged her.

Grandpa was out. Jerome and Willem staggered around the coffin in the truckbed. The leafsprings creaked. Dad yelled at Willem. "No, no, you idiot, we can't slide him out of the canvas. Goddamnit, what if he doesn't come out straight? He won't fit if he's cock-eyed in the box. Just set him down, goddamnittohell." The two-by-fours rested on the coffin ends. Grandpa swayed in the sling over the coffin. Jerome shoved more wild mint in his nose.

Dad's voice was just short of breaking. "We'll have to bury him in the canvas. There's no way we'll get the sling out from under him. We can't risk him flipping over." He yelled at Grandma, "We don't want to bury him *face down*, do we?"

"Do what you have to. Better buried in canvas than face down, I guess. Just get it over with."

The coffin wasn't long enough for the two-by-fours, so Dad stood, one leg in the coffin, hacking at them with a saw. First one end dropped then the other. Grandpa was in the coffin along with the two-by-fours and the canvas.

Grandma didn't want the smell of mothballs in the church, so Dad and Jerome broke and crushed the bunches of wild mint I had collected for the inside of the coffin. The smell of cedar and dusty mint mixed with the smell of death.

Dad put the top on the coffin and began to nail it down. He was using way too many nails. Even Grandma noticed. She smiled at me. "Don't worry, he won't get out." With her bony hand, she turned my face and stared into my eyes. "Josef, he was old and ready to die, and he got his way right to the end," she said. She pulled out four bottle caps out of her apron pocket. "Josef, I found these before Jerome saw them."

"But, Grandma," I cried, "I didn't want him to die. I was trying to be good to him. I just didn't think it would kill him."

"It wasn't you, Josef. He did it himself. Remember that." She put her arms around me and pulled me on her lap.

Sunlight pierced the Sacred Heart window and left a shaft of incense trailing in its wake. The smooth wooden box that held Grandpa's body rested on a velvet-draped stand. Six tall beeswax candles flanked the coffin, three to a side. They seemed to float above the ebony and silver candlesticks. It was hot and my knee quivered as if it would give way. A trickle of sweat ran down to the hollow of my back. Somehow, it looked cooler over by the huge coffin.

Father Reiter, the new young priest, never did one thing at a time. He pushed aside the gate of the communion rail with his foot as he adjusted the black vestment that flowed down from his shoulders. Before he had stepped from the platform he began,"Enternotintojudgementwithyour servantLord,forinyoursightnomanshallbejustifiedunlessYougranthim remissionofallhissins." Sweat trickled past the metal bows of his glasses and down his cheek. Through the open side of his vestment, dark stains of sweat showed.

The air hung like a bag over my head. Father Reiter added grains of incense to the glowing coals in the metal censer. He whirled into the incense cloud and disappeared. I'd never seen anyone use so much. His left hand held the chain, his right swung the incense holder as if driving out devils."DelivermeLordfromeverlastingdeathInthatawfuldayWhentheheavensandtheEarthshallbemovedWhenyouwillcometojudgetheEarthby fire." I couldn't wait to get outside in the fresh hot air.

At the cemetery everyone made the sign of the cross over the coffin with holy water. Grandpa's beautiful coffin was lowered into the ground with heavy ropes. The quiet procession to the cemetery straggled back talking, smiling even, chuckling at some remark. Ahead of us the men's society marched under the red *Männerverein* banner that swayed on its pole. The gold fringe flapped in a little breeze. All eyes turned to the west but there was no rain in it. Grandpa never did see the end of the drought. But it would end, just like everything else.

Empty-Handed

Over the years, we had many cats but few had names: they were working parts of the farm. *Stup-schwanz'*, meaning bobtail, is one name I remember. He was a spotted cat whose tail had been cut off by a sickle blade while mousing in the meadow near the house. Cats were useful. They worked for their living. The little milk they got from the strainer was a gift.

As a rule my mother did not allow animals in the house. She liked keeping things separate and in their place—people in, animals out. For a while, though, an orange cat slipped in. Under the table, his back arched beneath my bare foot. Then he would turn, and his thick furry tail would find its way between my four-year-old toes. I could feel his wide cheeks and whiskers rub against the insides of my feet. Four of us kids sat on the plank bench my father had made. Through a knothole in the plank, I would drop bits of fat to my favorite. Sometimes my sisters tattled or my mother would catch me and her eyes narrowed in a level stare.

One warm afternoon my great-uncle Payter came to visit in his black hat and newly-painted car. This was shortly after World War II, when no cars had been made for years. He was very proud of the shiny paint and we all went to look at it. We laughed as our faces, reflected in the curves of the fenders, would stretch like rubber. Even the Minnesota license plate looked shiny-new.

Onkel Payter was old, nearly eighty. I thought of him as useless, the way he'd ride around in his fancy car. What did he ever do but sit on the edge of his chair, his back as straight as a broom, his hands resting on his cane, his mustache twitching below his long nose? Onkel Payter and my mother bappelt on and on about relatives, potato bugs and the rain, and as my great-uncle sat waiting for his coffee to get cold, my orange cat jumped through the open door onto his lap. Onkel Payter yelped and half stood. He would have fallen backwards had the wall not been behind his chair. He looked at my mother and said, "Alvina!" I had never heard anyone speak sharply to my mother. She ordered me to take the cat out. When I came back, they both stopped talking at once and looked slyly at each other.

"*Ja, Mättis, mein Bubchen,*" my great-uncle said from under his mustache, in that voice people use talking to a four-year-old. "I need a cat. I want to buy your cat." I stared at him. His gold watch chain sparkled. He held a coin up to my face. "Here, take it, a shiny penny for your cat." I shook my head. He held it out arm's length and squinted at it. "*S'doch nei, gel?* But it's new, see?" He moved his thumb nail up under the number and read: "*Neunzehn hundert siebenundvierzig.* 1947."

I shook my head. *Nein.* His bushy black eyebrows went up and my mother glared at me. From the stove, she handed me a burnt frying pan and two baby bottles and told me to clean them.

I went outside and pumped some water into the bottles and the pan from the well pump and carried them to the fine sand that collected in the shallow depression by the driveway ditch. I put a little sand in the bottles and shook them, then poked at the crusty milk with a stick. The sun was shining in my face. I held a bottle up and squinted. When I had laid the clean bottles aside, I put sand in the iron pan and started to scrape it with one of the flat stones next to me. Brown streaks appeared in the black pan where I scraped. I was doing something useful.

My mother and Onkel Payter came around the corner of the house. She was carrying a thirty dozen egg case, holding it out in front of her, as if it were empty. The case bucked wildly in her hands and my mother bit at her lip as she tried to hold it steady. I thought I could hear my cat. Onkel Payter opened the car door. My mother set the case on the seat, then hurried back into the house. My great-uncle shuffled across the yard toward me. I could see his closed hand approach, his hairy knuckles unclench, his hand open, his wrist turn in his black sleeve. His mustache twitched. There was a flash of silver.

"*Zehn,*" he said. "Ten zent." The silver clattered in the iron pan.

"*Nein*, I don't want it," I cried. He turned and walked to the car and I shouted at his black shoulders, "Not for a hundred dollars."

He started the car, raced the engine then drove around the knoll of the well pump. He slowed and looked down his long nose at me.

"*Nein*," I said. I threw his dime against the window. It fell to the sand. I reached down for a heavy stone, stood up and heaved it at the car. It hit with a dull clunk. The glassy surface of the door buckled: I couldn't see myself in it anymore. His eyebrows arched up to his black hat. Another heavy stone. Clunk. The car stuttered as he stepped on the gas. Now a flat one. Clunk. I was out of stones.

I ran alongside but I wasn't tall enough to see the egg case in the back seat. I chased the car across the hot road, throwing gravel, handsful of gravel, that bounced and sprayed off the shiny black trunk like buckshot. *Nein, nein,* I shouted. The sharp stones cut into my feet. I ran until I couldn't see the shiny car anymore. I turned and walked home through the hot gravel, empty-handed.

Why Not the Train?

"Come home, Mama, come home now." Gerhard's fingers tightened around the toy locomotive in his palm. He put the toy on the quilt, chugging it over his chest. From the road, the headlights of an approaching car shone through the trees outside the window and threw spidery shadows on the wall above his head. That's her, Gerhard thought, she'd been at Alvina's, after all. The tires sounded on the washboarded road and the room fell dark. It wasn't her. He imagined himself on the train. Under his breath, he tooted the train's horn. Other mothers stayed home at night. Why didn't she? He wished she hadn't taught herself to drive.

In the bedroom below, the closet door opened and a chair scraped the floor. Gerhard heard the scratch of the tin box as Magnus took it from the shelf. Gerhard knew what his stepfather was doing. Once before, when his mother hadn't come home, he had crept down the stairs and through the lock had spied him reaching for the key he kept around his neck. Magnus took out the papers the banker had brought; then took out double-hands-full of greenbacks and hefted them, as gently as he might have lifted the udder of a favorite heifer. Magnus put the money on the bed and he began to count, wetting his hard, blackened thumb, the better to separate the slippery bills.

Gerhard remembered an earlier quarrel, after his mother had come home late. In his mind, the murmur of voices that suddenly broke into violent exchanges would forever be tied to the money that lay on the bed.

His eyes closed, until a car door slammed. Footsteps crunched on the gravel. The outhouse door opened and the coiled spring slammed it shut again. He wondered if she had been in the saloons in Spring Hill. He crept out of his bed and tiptoed into the room where his Aunt Agnes slept when she came back from the home for the retarded. The floor felt warm to his bare feet. He knelt and peeked through the grate in the floor that brought heat up from the kitchen.

"*Suzanna, wo warst du dann?*" Magnus's voice rang out, echoing into Agnes's room. He looked at his young wife as she tugged at her coat. She returned his look, the taste of whiskey in her mouth.

"*Besoffen bist du.* You weren't at Alvina's. You were at Meinulph's saloon. You're drunk."

"What do you care? It's not like one of your cows jumped the fence." Suzanna spat the words at him as she brushed back a strand of black hair. She threw her coat to the floor and advanced on him. "You bastard, you. Three thousand for a canopy for the Blessed Sacrament and I'm still sitting in a cold shithouse? You gave *three thousand dollars* to the church?"

Gerhard pulled back from the edge of the grate, as if afraid Magnus's sharp eyes could pierce the ceiling. That Magnus had bought the Blessed Sacrament canopy surprised him. Love and hate collided in his throat at the sound of his stepfather's voice.

"Where did you hear that?" Magnus stared at Suzanna.

"What difference does it make where I heard it? It's true, isn't it? Say it. You gave three thousand dollars to the priest last year—while I scrimped and saved for Gerhard's Communion clothes. A canopy with gold thread! You and your damn money . . . your God and your goddamned money."

"That's none of your business. You be home when it's supper. And look at me when I'm talking to you."

Suzanna turned back, holding the edge of the table for support. "I've had enough of you. You're no holier than the rest of us. But you treat us like dirt. Gerhard running around in rags, not going to school whenever you think you can get some work out of him."

"You keep out of my business. When I need him, he stays home. That's all there is to it. You didn't have to come here."

"And you didn't have to ask me." She mocked his voice. "Don't think you weren't getting something out of it. And don't think I didn't see you watching me across the line-fence." She looked around the primitive kitchen, at the cracked cast iron stove, and the hand pump that brought water up from the cistern. Magnus refused to improve the house his luckless father had left him. "You never gave a shit about me or Gerhard either. Admit it. Your mother died and you needed someone to do for you, someone to live in this shack, while you cozied up to the church."

Magnus stared out of the window, his hand resting on the dry rot of the windowsill. "I took you in," he said in a careful, even tone, "because you were with child, and didn't know which the father was. I took you in to preserve your honor and to make a home for your son . . ."

". . . preserve my honor? You liar! And it was *one* man I was with." Her voice cracked. "I'd be better off whoring in the Cities if that's what you think. At least that's honest work . . ."

Magnus whirled from the window. "You will not speak those words in my house. I took you in—when others would have hounded you out. You have a place here. People respect me and respect you in turn . . ."

". . . because they're blind or stupid or both." Suzanna's voice rose in anger. "There's nothing between us. All we share is the same Goddamn leaky roof. All you want is land and money. You care more for your cows than you do for me or my son."

"I made a home for him."

"Made a home for my son?" Suzanna laughed. "You treat him like a criminal. He's just a child." She picked up her coat and hung it on a nail. The coat fell and she kicked at it. "He's eight, Magnus. You work him like a hired man."

"You coddle the boy. He needs to be kept busy. You know idle hands are the devil's workshop. Besides, the boy likes to work."

"You idiot, Magnus, what do expect him to do? He's afraid of you." She turned away again. Magnus's anger rose to his face. He had long since given up expecting gratitude; a semblance of respect would have satisfied the unspoken code about wives that had been handed down to him by his father and his father's father.

He stared at Suzanna's straight back and slender white neck. At this moment, he remembered their wedding night, the sexual guilt he felt even within the bonds of marriage. She had driven a wedge under the hard shell of his discipline. *She* was his downfall and somehow, he didn't know how yet, Gerhard was in danger too.

He took a quick step across the floor and grasped her by the back of her neck. "Face me when you talk. You hear?" Suzanna whirled, knocked his hand down and pushed him back. "Keep your hands off me." His hand reached out and circled her neck. She pushed it away. "Let go of me!" He grabbed her neck again, hitting a nerve that shot pain down her back. She pulled away, losing her balance as she did. Magnus pushed her to the floor.

Suzanna rolled away from him toward the cupboard, and her hand groped in a drawer for her chicken knife. The fleeting image of a rooster's comb quivering under her shoe came back to her. In her mind she gave the feathered body a twist and forced the knife through the sinewy flesh of the neck.

She stood and shoved the knife at him. "Get back. Don't you touch me, Magnus. Get back, I said." Gerhard saw Magnus's hand dart out to grab the knife. Gerhard scrambled across the grate as they moved out of his line of sight, his heart pounding. The muscles in his right arm knotted with anticipation.

They grappled, Magnus pounding Suzanna's hand against the cistern pump. They separated then clashed again. Gerhard rose up in fear, then knelt again, as together Magnus and Suzanna fell heavily to the kitchen floor. Magnus stood up with the knife in his hand. He stared at the darkening sleeve of his shirt. "You cut me, you whore." He groped for the handkerchief in his pocket. "You cut me!"

Suzanna rose to her feet and staggered outside, slamming the door. She hesitated on the step, then ran for the car. Gerhard hurried from the grate to his own bedroom window and saw her close the car door and start the engine. She was leaving without him.

She opened the door and shouted up at his window. "I'll come back for you, Gerhard, I will." Magnus ran, clutching his bleeding arm. He grabbed the door and dragged her out by the hair.

"*Hure!* I'll teach you to cut." In a fury, he struck at her, locked her head in the crook of his arm and slammed her head repeatedly against the car door. She slumped and he dragged her the short distance to the corncrib. He pushed her inside and slammed it shut. He ran to the shed, returning with hammer and nails, and nailed the door shut. Panting, he peered through the slats at Suzanna's form.

He grabbed the keys and, despite his fury, he returned the hammer to its place then walked to the house, hand tight to his sleeve.

He sat at the scarred kitchen table and bandaged his arm, amazed at the turn his life had taken. It had been Magnus's fevered imaginings that there had been other young men. Magnus had resigned himself to a life of celibacy until he found he was attracted to the slim, black-haired girl who could be seen working in his neighbor's field. After hurried meetings with Suzanna's parents, Magnus's interest and the size of his land holdings swung the balance in his favor. Later he cursed his weakness. He confessed his impure thoughts to the priest and punished his body's unruly hunger. He hoped his desires could be somehow sanctified within the bonds of marriage.

Gerhard crept back to his bed and lay rigid under the cold covers, fearing the angry tread on the stair. His lips moved silently, repeating the few words that could drive other thoughts from his mind. *Bitt' für uns. Bitt' für uns Sündern . . .* "Pray for us. Pray for us sinners." The cold of the room seeped into him and the edges of the locomotive bit into his hand. It was his fault, being born.

He thought of what he had heard, that Magnus had bought the canopy for the procession of the Blessed Sacrament. He recalled Father Reiter carrying the heavy gold monstrance with the sacred Host, surrounded by four men holding the four mahogany poles (people said, *bound in shining brass*, a new canopy of creamy-white silk with gold thread, *real gold*, it was repeated, with the Holy Ghost in the form of a dove hovering above creamy white clouds). So that's how Magnus got to carry the right front pole of the canopy.

Gerhard slept fitfully and dreamed of a sun that floated into darkness then rose again a vibrating yellow ball in a blue sky. He was a grown-up. He had a long robe like St. Francis, held around his waist with a soft knotted rope. It swayed above his sandaled feet. The air was warm and moist, moving gently from the grove of palm trees. This is where he would go. In the distance, he heard the babble of laughing children grow louder and he saw their smiling faces and waving arms. He was a priest, sent to care for them. A soft breeze caressed his face and the sweet full smell of strange flowers filled the air. Then a cloud passed over the sun and the wind blew cold.

That night Suzanna woke and felt blood-encrusted hair pasted to her forehead. She lay among the horizontal bars of moonlight on the floor. Stiffly she rose and went to the door. Reaching through the slats, she opened the hasp and pushed at the door, but it would not give. The cold strips of light and dark wavered on her hand as she tested each slat on the inside of the crib. The crib was stronger than it looked. In desperation, she took off her shoes and climbed the slats to the peak. There, a vented door creaked open. She retrieved her shoes and climbed over the cold ledge of the door to freedom. She went to the barn, then ran down the moonlit gravel road wrapped in a reeking horse-blanket. She thought furiously of her past. How she and Magnus had married at the parish house, witnessed only by her parents, who then banished her from their lives. Scorn was all she could expect from them or any of her sisters. Too late now. You made your bed, now lie in it.

She decided to go to the ramshackle house that stood on one of Magnus's farms near the river bridge. It was at a farmer's house near this river she had worked as a hired girl. Along its shaded banks *die Knechten,* the hired men, would gather for their weekly baths on summer Saturday nights, carefully placing at the base of a tree, the cracked porcelain saucers that held a generous slice of homemade laundry soap furnished by the woman of the house. The smell of the tallow-and-lye soap did not conceal the musky odor of men in their prime.

It was here that Suzanna and her *Knecht* arranged to meet, under the arms of a great basswood that stood upstream from the bathing hole. Despite the faithful lighting of votive candles before the statue of the Virgin, Suzanna was finally betrayed by the moon that shone like liquid on the bark of the basswood and the ivory of her shoulders. At the end of summer, she discovered she was pregnant. Her *Knecht* disappeared.

Exhausted, Suzanna stumbled down the lane to the abandoned farmstead. In the moonlight, the boards of the house shone a luminous gray behind the overgrown tangle of the yard. The back door gave way with one thrust of her shoulder. She lay on the dusty floor wrapped in the smell of horses. She would decide in the morning what she would do.

The next morning, Gerhard woke at the sound of Magnus's boots on the stairs. His stepfather bent his head for the low door and came into Gerhard's room. He stared down at his stepson. "She's gone and good riddance. Now you'll take care of the chickens. For the hogs, start that load of corn. It's almost light. Get going."

Gerhard walked toward the pig yard next to the busch, his eyes intent on the empty corncrib where Magnus had put his mother. The small door at the top of the crib hung open. The car was still nearby. He wondered if someone from the saloons had come for her. The thought of Magnus's bleeding arm made him hurry.

That long day, Gerhard waited in vain for some sign of his mother. Magnus did not let him out of his sight. They drove the forty miles to retrieve his sister from the home. Agnes would cook and clean for them. They rode in grim silence, in a drizzle that became a driving rain mixed with pellets of ice. Gerhard listened to the rattle of the sleet on the windshield and watched Magnus out of the corner of his eye.

Looking at the river farm and its shabby house, Magnus recalled how his unruly brothers and sisters rebelled against him when he decided to buy it. His weak mother had given up and it had become Magnus's job to discipline them. As soon as they were able, all but Agnes fled to the city, but not before Magnus had sweated out every ounce of fat in their unwilling bodies. In the ten years since the beginning of the Great Depression, he had bought many other farms, expanding the barns, hiring men, and increasing the size of the herds to take advantage of his neighbors' misfortunes.

The next day, All Saints' Day, began gray and bitterly cold. All Souls' Day that followed promised no better. Gerhard again woke to the sound of footsteps on the stairs. "Get up, it's already light. First chores then church. See that you fill those chicken feeders to the top." Magnus turned and was gone.

The wagonload of corn still stood next to the fence. His first job was to throw the daily corn to the pigs. With each jabbing motion of the shovel, the stiff rubber tires of the trailer rocked in the muddy ruts. A single crow flapped across the broad frost-covered valley. With a downward swoop, the black form slowed then rose again to land on the pointed finger of an oak. Gerhard straightened his back to look, then glanced hurriedly over his shoulder. He didn't know if she would come for him or was he to escape on his own. He pondered why she had left him with the man she hated. He didn't know what to do. To calm himself, he repeated the words again and again. *Bitt' für uns, Bitt' für uns.*

Behind him, in the metal-gray sky, the sun hung green and silent. Before him, past the edge of the barn, lay the half-harvested cornfield, its broken stalks bent in submission to the cold iron of the rattling corn picker. In his face, the wind blew a mist that coated the bill of his cap and stiffened the gnarled trees of the dying windbreak. At his feet, behind the mended and remended wooden fence, a grunting herd of pink-nosed, squealing pigs fought over frozen ears of corn that lay scattered among the iron heaps of pig manure. The green light of the sun glittered briefly on the copper rings embedded in the hard rims of their flat noses. To be as unfeeling, as mindless as the rooting of the pigs: that was his wish.

His left hand, its thumb bared to the rusted iron socket of the shovel, fell open, and the corn spilled. With a thin-soled shoe, he levered the shovel back into the pile and drove it home with a savage thrust. The edge of the shovel caught on splintered wood and the handle drove deep into his groin. As he fell into the corn, his head twisted and his eyes met the green circle of light in the sky.

From behind the hay stack came a tall thin figure. Magnus's sharp eyes looked out from under an overhang of black eyebrows. The windburn on his gaunt face masked the pallor of his thrice-weekly fasting. His head swiveled. His eyes traced the edge of the grove, the tired fence, the half-unloaded wagon of corn. His fist tightened on the five-tined fork in his hand. He spotted the boy half-hidden by the wagonsides. His long legs covered the distance. He raised the fork high and brought it down with a handle-splintering crash near the cleared space by the boy's head.

"*Scheiss-Arsch!* Get your hands out of there, you little shit-ass. You'll go to hell like your mother." The boy lurched to his feet. Magnus stared at the splintered handle in his stinging hand. "Look what you made me do," he said, "you'll pay with the strap." In his fury, he broke the shivered handle over his knee and knocked Gerhard's legs out from under him. "Finish up, *Kamelles-Kopf.* Agnes is waitin' breakfast on you. I'm going inside."

Gerhard finished, then hurried past the corncrib. At the crumbling steps of the house, he scraped the caked mud from his shoes. He hated to make more work for Agnes. When he opened the door, Agnes reached for the pitcher of batter and poured four pancakes on the black griddle on the stove. In a black pan, she turned two large sausages. She smiled at him and poured coffee into the chipped cup next to his plate.

"You cold, Gerhard?" She walked heavily toward him and cupped her warm hands over his ears. "*Die Ohren sind doch steif gefroren.* Where is your winter cap? Your ears are frozen, Gerhard."

Magnus opened the door of the bedroom. He glared at Agnes. She dropped her arms to her sides and turned back to the stove. Angrily Magnus pulled his chair across the uneven floor and sat. "Sit down." he said at Gerhard. Gerhard sat. They waited in silence, listening to the sizzle of the sausages in the pan. When the food was brought, Gerhard dared to warm his hands on his cup. Magnus stared at him but said nothing. Agnes turned to her brother. "Magnus, *ess doch,* eat some sausage. To work you need to eat."

Magnus smiled. "Thank you, Agnes. Only warm water for me. Remember, today is Wednesday, for me a fast day. Wednesday, Friday, and Saturday. Punish the body to win the soul . . ." he paused, ". . . and the souls of others."

When he had buried his mother, Magnus began to fear his own death. He developed unrelenting scruples that, in his case, infected even the few pleasures he allowed himself. He began to improve upon the regulations of the Church to salve his conscience.

He gave a tight smile and looked at Gerhard. Gerhard looked down at his plate. Even Agnes knows better than to punish the body, he thought. Magnus stared hungrily at Gerhard's plate.

"You give the boy too much, Agnes. It makes him lazy."

Agnes looked fondly at her brother and shook her head from side to side. "Gerhard big." She took Magnus's cup, raised the iron cover of the hot water reservoir in the stove and dipped the cup into the water. With her apron, she wiped the bottom of the cup and set it in front of her brother. Magnus stared at Agnes in disbelief then looked into the cup. He hid his distaste as he took the first sip. It tasted fuzzy, as if something were growing there. For penance, he drank it in a gulp. He decided he would return Agnes to the home after Mass.

All Souls' Day. Gerhard opened his eyes slowly. He had been dreaming of pigs; that pigs had invaded his bedroom, that pigs were schnaufing under his bed, hungry pigs, grinning up at him, with that half-smile all pigs have when they raise their heads above the horizontal. The air in his room felt cold and damp. He heard the pigs again. He hung over the side of his bed, looked under it, then ran for the window.

Outside, a gray fog pressed against the window. The sound of pigs came again, made louder by the dense fog. He could see nothing. Then, faintly, came the sound of a train whistle, a sound he had heard only twice before, each time carried over the distance of ten miles by a steady north wind. But today, the fog hung motionless before his eyes. There was no wind. In his mind, he saw the long line of cars roll by. It had to stop somewhere he could get on. If his mother would not come, he would go alone, on foot. He stood stock-still, until his legs ached, listening for the sound to repeat.

At six in the morning, the car picked its way through the fog toward the church. Gerhard rode in the back seat. He was hungry. Magnus had returned Agnes to the Home. Gerhard noticed he didn't get much food when Magnus was fasting. The fog hovered, giving back no light.

Magnus, somber and erect, drove with some anticipation. Of all the Holy Days, this was his favorite. He came early, because he preferred the morning solitude of the church to the crowded afternoon and evening. The kneeling and the repetition of the prayers pleased him. He swelled with the knowledge that with each visit, another soul was released from Purgatory solely through his intercession. In the back of his mind, he hoped, *nein*, he expected, that his own time in Purgatory would be shortened by his efforts.

Increasingly, the saving of souls had become entwined with the contents of the tin box. In recent years he returned from his devotion, and closing the door from Suzanna's eyes, yielded to the compulsion to recount his money, knowing full well the exact amount he had piled up toward his next land purchase. He put that thought out of his mind as he drove up to the church. He sat for a moment, his hand on the key in the ignition, and stared up at the great spire that soared upward from the crest of the hill, but now stood truncated by the heavy mist.

Magnus had walked half the short distance to the church when he realized that Gerhard was still in the car. *"Komm' doch."* He beckoned impatiently with his left arm, then touched the thick bandage under his sleeve. *"Komm."* As they climbed the granite steps to the great doors of the church, Magnus spoke.

"Remember now, Gerhard. Six Our Fathers, six Hail Marys, six Glory Bes and poof! another soul gets out of Purgatory and into heaven. You have to do it right. Six of each prayer, then go out, wait a bit, then back in and start all over. One soul each visit. *Versteh?* You have to leave the church and come back in, or it doesn't work."

The cold damp air had infiltrated the church. The stained-glass windows loomed gray in the half-light. The smell of incense overlay the odor of floorwax. The vaulted ceiling lay hidden in the gloom above, as if the fog had somehow penetrated the upper reaches of the church. The lamp that signaled God's presence flickered hesitantly behind its red glass. Only the yellow blaze of votive candles in front of the Virgin statue provided a corner of light and warmth in the silence of the church. Gerhard looked around. The church was empty, except for Mrs. Kreutzer with the bobbing head and her visiting sister.

As Magnus's footsteps sounded the way to his accustomed place, he idly counted the candles and multiplied their cost. He wondered who would light so many candles. He genuflected deeply and knelt in a pew that afforded a view of the locked cabinet where the canopy was kept. Gerhard chose a place opposite Magnus, on the left of the church, near the looming confessional, on a bench shortened by one of the great posts that supported the vaulted ceiling. He stared up at the statue of St. Francis. He would go alone.

Magnus began to pray while Gerhard hesitated, distracted in part by the lurid vision of Hell and Purgatory instilled in him by Sister Mary Benedict. Magnus had already saved one soul from suffering when Gerhard resorted to counting his prayers on his fingers and thumbs, so as not to lose his place. The door slammed as Magnus left after the first of the many visits he would make.

"Ssst, Sssst, Gerhard." His name sounded from the choir loft. He turned. In the semi-darkness he could make out a form in the loft above him. There was a silence and then the pad of hurried footsteps on the staircase behind him. Suzanna ran lightly toward him, shoes in hand, and embraced him awkwardly as he struggled to stand. She was still wearing the same dress she'd worn that night. Her hair stood out from her head, her eyes blazed feverishly and her mouth was twisted into a horrible smile.

"Where were you, Mama? I waited and waited."

"At the farm by the bridge. When he comes . . ."

He looked down at her feet. "Mama, you're barefoot in church."

Suzanna shook her head impatiently. "Listen, when he comes in," she whispered hoarsely into his ear, "when he comes in, you go out. See if the keys are in the car. That's the important thing. Or else we have to go on foot. See if . . ." The outside door opened again and Suzanna ducked behind the velvet curtain of the confessional. Gerhard knelt, his knees quivering uncontrollably.

At the sound of Magnus's heels echoing in the gloom, Gerhard glanced back. Magnus looked at him sternly and nodded, as if to tell him to get to business. Gerhard bent his neck, but then stood quickly. In his confusion, he genuflected to the back of the church. His face reddened as he fled the building, tugging desperately at the door in his haste. Sliding his hand along the cold iron railing, he ran down the wet granite steps and to the car. He stood on the running board and looked in. The keys were there. He opened the door, took them out, put them back, took them out again, and ran.

His breath came in short painful gasps that he did his best to hide. Holding his hand firmly on his leg to quiet the keys in his pocket, Gerhard returned to his place beside the great pillar. Magnus barely caught sight of him. Gerhard knelt, his shoulders tensed to the point of sharp pain. His mind leapt from fear of Magnus to fear of the twisted smile on his mother's face. He would never escape now. To calm himself he began his Our Fathers and Hail Marys and in his mind's eye, he saw himself writhing in the eternal flame. At the words, *Heilige Maria, Mutter Gottes, bitt' für uns Sündern,"* he heard a voice growing louder and louder, filling the empty church, in a chant that inexplicably rose from his own chest, *"Bitt für uns, BITT FÜR UNS SÜNDERN."* His knuckles whitened on the bench before him. His right hand went to his throat as if to stop the voice. He saw the heavy velvet curtain part and his mother's face appear. She reached her hand toward him and clamped it tightly over his mouth.

"*Ruhig!*," she hissed in his ear. She locked his head in the crook of her arm and dragged him out of the pew. Gasping for air, he half-stood then fell awkwardly back.

Magnus turned at the sound of the struggle.

"*Hur-re*," he roared. "You've come back, have you?" His anger rose to his face in a flush of heat. In the darkness of the church, the whites of Gerhard's eyes leapt out at him. He saw them as a call for help. Magnus stood in his confusion.

"Leave him, Suzanna. Leave us in peace. We don't want you anymore. He's better off with me."

He bounded across the aisle and into the opposing row of pews where he stumbled and fell forward in his haste. He cried out in pain. Mrs. Kreutzer and her sister stared but did nothing. He rose up from the benches to the sight of Suzanna's backing retreat. It was then that Gerhard's voice broke free of his mother's grip. *"Nein, Magnus, nein, nein, nein, und nochmal NEIN."*

Suzanna grabbed Gerhard's hand and they ran to the door and down the steps to the car. Magnus raced after them, his coat flying as he vaulted the slippery stairs. Suzanna jumped into the driver's seat, Gerhard into the back. "The keys, where are the keys?" she screamed. Gerhard fumbled in his pocket. Magnus's bony red face grew larger and larger until it was ready to engulf them both. The engine caught and the car lurched forward. Magnus's hand grasped the door handle, his foot searching blindly for the running board as he struggled to keep pace with the car. Suzanna twisted the wheel and pushed the accelerator to the floor. Magnus's feet left the ground. The pull on his hand was too great, and he skidded across the ground beside the car.

Suzanna raced through the fog back to the farm. Gerhard sat, as if stricken, in the back seat. She ran into the bedroom, pushed a chair into the closet and pulled the box from the shelf. "He won't be buying more land with this." she muttered. She took the quilt from the bed and ran to the stove, pushing it into the flames. It caught fire and she returned to the bedroom and threw the flaming quilt on the bed.

Again she returned to the stove, opened the lower door and scraped live coals into the ash bucket. With the box under one arm, the bucket in the other, she ran outside. She threw the box on the seat. "One more thing, Gerhard, one more." She ran to the haystack and began to pull great armloads of hay from the stack and piled them around the corncrib. The back door of the car opened. Gerhard joined her, taking hay to the barns by the dying windbreak then opening gates so the pigs could escape. Together they scattered the glowing coals in the hay then ran for the car.

"We did it, Gerhard, we did it." she cried. She held the box on her lap and started the car. "It's done," she repeated, "and I wish Magnus were here to see it. What would he think of that, Gerhard?"

"Are we free, Mama? Can we go to the train?" In the orange glow of flames leaping into fog, she drove twice around the yard. On her face, Gerhard saw her horrible look of satisfaction. He spoke again in a hesitant voice: "To the train, Mama. Let's go to the train."

Suzanna turned in her seat and threw him a riveting look. "Why not, Gerhard? Why not the train?"

Infinity

It is December and I am seven. I am throwing down hay for our livestock, which number thirty cows, an equal number of calves and by chance, an equal number of yearlings. It is dark. The single bulb in the haymow throws many shadows but scant light to work by. A shaft of dim light rises through the hole from the barn below, but shines uselessly against the dark rafters. Below me, I hear the hum of the milking machines, the rattle of stanchions, the mewing of cats by the milk strainer, and the bleat of a calf.

It is early winter and the sweet loose hay still reaches nearly to the rafters. It would be easy to lose my place, slide down the slippery hay and fall through the open hole to the concrete floor. The door leading to the barn below is opened only for throwing down hay, so the haymow is as cold as any attic might be with fifteen feet of insulation between it and the heat below.

As I pull a large clump of hay toward the hole and allow it to slide down the slope into the lower barn, particles of dust, dimly lit from below, rise like a column in the warm updraft. Usually I get away from the dangerous hole and the rising dust motes as quickly as possible, but I am struck by how much dust is coming from some marsh grass we'd cut in a rain-flooded slough. I stand on the slippery slope, dribbling small quantities of hay over the hole, trying to create as many dust particles as possible. I wonder how many could possibly be in any forkful. If I had a safer place to stand, I'm sure I could count them. I drag more of the hay to the hole. I realize that given enough time I could count all of the stems of hay in the entire haymow, though seen all at once it looks impossible. I think of stacking all the hay in piles of five stems and counting them. I think of all the hay that had been in the mow the year before, and the year before that and then all the way back to 1910 when the barn was built. I'm sure I could count them, although I think I would lose interest.

I think of all the drops of milk this hay could produce; adding of course, the myriad drops of water brought up from the well by the windmill from the long rivers that must run under the earth. But still, given enough time, even these drops could be counted, along with all the raindrops that fell on our farm this year and last and way back to when Grandpa Schuler owned this farm and then even when there were just Indians and even before them. They could all be counted. As I look up at the dim bulb that burns overhead, I see my breath and I think of all the little pieces of air that go into my nose and then come back out again, and of all the yeasty air from the warm fat cows below, and these too, I realize, could be counted; and the huge lakes of air that churn over our farm and the air that goes all the way across the state, even around the world and these too could be counted.

I finish throwing down and think of the deep snow on the ground that separates the barn from the house and of the number of snowflakes. Not for one second do I believe that they are all different, as if God had nothing better to do with His time. But they are countable. When the last one was set aside or melted on my fingertip, I would know the exact number, which could be written, even if the number stretched all the way to the North Pole.

By this time the milking is finished. My brother starts feeding the hay I've thrown down and my father scrubs the milking machines with his good hand. The milk separator divides the cream from the skim. After I scrape the concrete floor behind the gutters and spread lime over the wet spots, my father tells me I can go.

I open the barn door. Subzero air hits my lungs. I look across the long, long expanse of hard-packed snow toward the house, which looks lost amid the high snowbanks. I walk with my eyes on my feet, listening to the snow squeal, each snowflake in pain as I put my weight on it. I do not look up. I tell myself I will not look up this time. I listen to the agony of the snow, brittle edge set against neighboring jagged tooth, until I can stand it no longer. I throw a quick glance upward, at a fierce black sky turned almost white by winter stars all staring down. I walk faster but the house recedes in the distance. The expanse of fearsome stars reaches from horizon to horizon. I begin to run and the sounds of my pounding foot-steps echo above the screaming snow. I look up and run even faster. I am not gaining ground but am continually at a spot halfway to the house. I remain frozen in that space, still halfway to the house, in a terror of the uncountable things that glare from the sky above. I run as hard as I can and still half-way, my face is cocked at the heavens as if I were being drawn upwards, where God Himself is manifest in all His Terror. Above me, the huge grinding of the sky throws off jagged shards, the strings from my earflaps whip at my face and I run, my face locked toward the sky, my eyes fixed on the stars.

Juletta and Josef

It is deep winter, 1951, in central Minnesota, when relentless storms sweep the rolling landscape of small farms and woodlots, obliterating the usual landmarks with shifting, dizzying waves of drifting snow. The short days are half the length of the long nights and staying in the house is hardly better than leaving. The harsh bite of winter binds the men to their barns and cattle; the women to their kitchens and children.

It is deep winter, when even a heavy coat at Sunday Mass fails to warm the wearer but rather serves to insulate him from his neighbor. On St. Blaise Day, the church overflows with fathers and mothers and their eight children or more, the old and the young. Even those burdened with sin and guilt can approach the altar without shame and for a brief moment, feel part of a larger, living body. Wind-burned faces crowd the Communion rail to have the priest bless their throats with the smooth fragrance of the two crossed beeswax candles of St. Blaise. The parish prays in unison to the Saint to protect them from maladies of the throat, from colds and inflammations, from coughs and swelling and, in the memories of the older survivors, for protection from the scourges of influenza and diptheria that filled row upon row upon row of graves in the evergreen-clad graveyard behind the church.

Juletta wet her finger on her tongue and touched the bottom of the large flatiron in her hand. There was no sizzle. The blue light of midwinter entered the south windows. She tucked a stray hair behind her ear. The weight of the heavy wedge of metal made her wince. A sharp pain in her elbow reminded her of her fall with an armful of frozen clothes from the line. She put the flatiron on the stove and slid out the handle. She stared at the other two already on the stove. She always mixed them up. East one cold, she repeated to herself, east one cold, east one cold. She tried the new iron with her finger. Too hot. She didn't want to scorch his good Sunday shirt. East one cold. Waiting for the iron to cool, she stared at the gold band on her coarse hand. She looked away, up at the crucifix on the wall, at the thin cool body with outstretched arms that glowed white against the black wooden cross. He was the only other man she'd seen this close to naked. East one cold.

Juletta saved the easy ironing for last: the girls' blouses, big red handkerchiefs, the kids' everyday ones, her tatted lacy Sunday one. She moved fast, before the heat dissipated into the cool air. Above her lip, in the fine hair visible only when sidelit by the unblinking snow, the first beads of sweat began to form. West one hot. From the unheated bedroom behind her, a draft numbed her ankles, leaving her feet wooden, like the backs of old scrub brushes. She recalled the thick warm walls of the house where she had worked as a hired girl. Stefan Ernt, just a year older, had followed her through the big house as she did her work. How easily she could have married up rather than down. The Ernts had taken advantage of the price increases and their grain elevators expanded along the tracks. She blushed at these thoughts in the blue winter light of her kitchen.

Florence, her four-year-old, was at her in-laws' for the day. On the couch in the front room, five-year-old Eberhard turned and groaned in his sleep. In the night, he had complained of his stomach, sitting up to relieve the pain. Her husband Josef had slept through it, turning only once when Ebbie cried out. When Josef took Beatrice and Sarah to school, he'd left Flo at his mother's house. She was grateful for that much.

She hated the name Beatrice. Josef had insisted on it. West one hot. Juletta suspected it was the name of an old girlfriend from New Munich. The west one was not hot, the east one was not hot. She lifted the stove lid. A gray ash lay at the center of the firebox, like the dottle of a pipe. She wiped at her eyes. The fire had gone out for the first time all winter.

She lifted the cover of the woodbox and stared at the scraps at the bottom. She reached down and rose in time to catch a glimpse of a horse's rump and Josef gliding by the porch window. He was standing on the sled; the children sat huddled under the horse blanket, only their heads showing. Juletta lit the pieces of bark with a match from the tin matchbox which hung next to the stove. As she waited for the flame to rise, she studied the scene painted on the tin box—skaters on a pond surrounded by tall buildings. The girls wore fur hats and muffs, the boys short jackets and long scarves that dangled almost to their knees. Perfect puffs of breath hung before their smiling faces. She recalled where this matchbox had hung in her mother's warm kitchen.

The door opened. Sarah and Bea crashed into the kitchen on a wave of cold that crossed the floor. They pulled off coats and scarves and sat on the floor to unbuckle their overshoes. "Ma," Sarah blurted out, "this morning when I got to school my nose was frozen to my scarf."

"What did I tell you?"

"Mama! I'm not going to wear an old *vindel* over my nose no matter how cold it gets. The other kids will laugh at me."

"Don't be silly, Sarah, it's a clean white piece of cloth. It *used to be* a diaper; but it's warm soft cotton. Is Papa bringing Flo in?"

"Mama! we forgot to stop at Grandma's to get Flo." Bea shouted. "Boy, is Papa going to get it." The door opened again and Josef's dark hair and frosty black mustache poked through. He flipped his heavy cap through the air and missed the hook.

"Josef, *wo ist die Flo?*"

Josef stammered, "Juletta, I was daydreaming and drove right by." He held his earlobes to warm them. How could I have forgotten, he thought. Now the fur'll fly. "I even waved at Grandpa," he said. "So that's what he was yelling about. I didn't want to turn around, the way he bapples on and on. We'd have froze." His cheek flushed through the windburn on his face. He looked so sheepish Juletta had to turn away. She was trying not to find fault so much.

"That's all right, Josef. She'll still be there in the morning. Just bring her back when you take the kids to school. Now that they have a telephone I can call Grandma and tell her what happened."

"Juletta, you have any coffee?" He touched the cold pot and turned to her. "*S'doch kalt.* Since when do you let the fire go out in the middle of the day?"

"I was daydreaming too. I just relit it. I'll bring in some wood."

Josef went into the front room. "How's my Ebbie doing now?" Ebbie was sitting up, holding the blanket around his stomach, "*Mein Bauch, es tut noch Weh, Papa.*"

"Your belly still hurts? *Wo dann?* Here? Lower?" He called over his shoulder, "Juletta, come here." He looked up. "What do you make of this, it hurts way down there." Juletta opened the buttons on his long underwear. She sighed, and moved the small bag of skunk fat Josef had pinned to the underwear. Ebbie pointed to a spot just above his tiny penis.

Juletta sighed again. "Don't you remember, Josef? That's the same place he complained about before. Do you think we should take him back to Doctor Gans?"

Josef shook his head, "Waste of three dollars. He didn't do anything last time. He'll feel better after supper."

Juletta's eyes scanned Josef's face. He looked away. Skunk fat.

The next morning, the nail heads in the girls' upstairs closet were white with frost. The depressions in the snow glowed like blue dimples in the morning light. Bea and Sarah pulled on woolen stockings by the open oven. Ebbie moaned on a blanket by the wood stove. Juletta stood by the kitchen door, holding a scarf to tie over the diaper around Sarah's neck. "It'll keep you warm. Pull it off before you get to school and no one will notice."

Josef's cheeks were bright red when he came into the kitchen. Juletta could feel the cold radiating from his coat. "It's getting worse, Josef. He's hardly eaten in three days. He can't live on crackers and cold coffee; he's getting a lump there." She pulled the mittens over Bea's little hands. Expectantly, she turned to stare at Josef's blank expression. "Say *some* thing, would you?"

Startled, Josef jumped. "Oh, *ja*. Well. I'll ask the folks."

"Sure," Juletta mumbled. "More skunk fat." She tied Sarah's scarf. "Remember, take it off before you get to school. And tell Mrs. Timlich to slide the desks back to the stove if you get too cold."

Sarah pouted. "We did yesterday and I still had to wear my mittens for penmanship."

Juletta filled the bread bowl from the tin-lined flour bin. She recalled Sarah sitting on the porch steps last summer, her elbow in a washbasin full of steaming cowshit. Josef had waited in the cow yard for an hour before he marched to the house, as proud as a new bride with a cake. It had to be fresh, he pronounced, or the ringworm wouldn't go away. Sarah cried and held her nose. Juletta had laughed, but was stunned when the circle went away.

The snow had stopped but the wind swirled around the oaks, deepening the dark wells around each trunk. She checked the clock to make sure the news was over; she couldn't bear to hear any more about Korea. Her cousin Romuald had been sent there in October. She tried to imagine the Chinese invading the south, realizing she'd never even heard of Korea or the Chinese two years earlier. She smoothed the small quilt over the dough, then went to Ebbie who cried out. She held him in her arms.

When Ebbie dozed off, Juletta put on her heavy coat and scarf and hurried to the smokehouse to bring in meat. She returned, her outstretched arms heavy with rings of frozen sausage. She caught sight of the horses as they cleared the horizon at the highway.

Flo bounded into the kitchen, "Ma, it was fun, can I stay with them again tonight?" Josef unhitched the team and led them to the barn. The car sat useless in the shed. The county said the roads would be plowed this year but the plows were no match for the seventy inches of snow that had fallen so far. Josef spent a lot of time on the sled, going the two and a half miles to and from school.

He slapped his cap against his leg and a fine shower of snow melted as it hit the floor. Josef rubbed his hands. "How's my Ebbie?" he asked.

"He just fell asleep when you drove in. It's still the same: he whimpers in his sleep and cries when he wakes. The lump looks bigger. I don't know what to think. Should I call Dr. Gans?"

"I wouldn't waste a long distance call. What can he say on the phone he didn't say before in person?"

Juletta answered quickly. "We have to decide, Josef."

"Well," he said cautiously, "Grandma says it could be the *Därm* pushing out. If the gut breaks in there, it's like poison." Josef hesitated, then took a deep breath. "They thought maybe if we took him to the *Hexe* by the railroad track . . ."

"What? Poison . . . and they're talking about some Gypsy?" Her voice rose. "Your family! For your own son?"

Josef sat by the door and picked at the frozen ice in his overshoe buckles with his fingernails. "Juletta, remember when Uncle Martin lost his hand to the cornpicker? That first winter, his missing hand kept freezing even though it wasn't there? Well, she hypnotized him and put a mitten on it for him and it never bothered him again." Juletta thought of chickens lying in sand, hypnotized by a line scratched in the gravel by naughty boys.

"Your family will believe anything. Grandpa taking off warts with that looping string . . ." Juletta blushed. "How is tying a loose knot around a wart supposed to do anything? What difference would it make holding up the string and lighting it to see if the knot burns . . . ?" She laughed. ". . . and why would the wart be gone by the first full moon?" She laughed again, uneasily.

"What could be simpler?" Josef asked.

Juletta glanced at the front room as Ebbie whimpered again. "Can't we take him to the hospital?"

Josef looked away. "I suppose. But we can't get the car out. And Uncle Martin's truck isn't up by the highway. He must have been caught at home by this last storm. Thirteen miles is too far to drive horses in this weather." Wind rattled the bedroom windows. Josef looked at Juletta and turned on the radio.

"Josef, we can't just sit here. I hate it when you keep putting things off. If it's so bad, why are the girls at school?" Juletta's voice shook. She knew she shouldn't question her husband. Ebbie cried and she went into the front room. He was holding his stomach again. She tried to recompose her face. "Do you want anything to eat, Ebbie? *Butterbrot*, wouldn't that be nice, or crackers?" His tiny face contorted in pain and tears filled his eyes. Juletta hurried from the room.

"We've got to . . ."

"Ruhig." Josef held his hand up and stared at the radio.

" . . . *high winds tonight, extending across the eastern Dakotas, gradually moving across all of Minnesota, continuing snow through tomorrow, temperatures to remain moderate through the night with a low of eleven below.*"

"Josef, it'll get worse. Let's do something now."

"OK. OK. What if I call Hafner to bring his plow around from the west? The snow isn't as deep on the back side of the section. We can get the car out that way. We could be at the hospital this afternoon."

With her good butcher knife, Juletta sliced the bread dough and formed the eight loaves. She turned on the radio again. Polkas, advertising, more Chinese Communists, finally the weather. Nothing had changed, only the level of excitement in the announcer's voice. Ebbie wanted to be held. The lump was even larger. Josef looked into the front room. "The car's running. I'll feed the stock now."

She thought of how she had spurned Stefan Ernt's advances. She remembered Mrs. Ernt's disappointment and her repeated requests to stay on. How welcome were Josef's careful attentions. How quickly love had blossomed between them.

Josef came back into the house. Juletta looked at him.

"No, I don't know why he isn't here," Josef answered irritably. "I climbed halfway up the windmill but I couldn't see a thing. He could be a hundred feet from the busch and we wouldn't know it. That damn forecast's way off. The storm is here now. I'll call Getchell's again and see when he left."

Josef's voice suddenly turned hard. "Put him on then . . ."

He listened intently, his eyes on the silver bells above the speaker. He hung up the phone. "That's that," he said. He turned to Ebbie. "Can you wait, Ebbie? It doesn't hurt as much anymore, does it?" Ebbie shook his head, "It hurts more, Papa." His eyes drifted from side to side.

"Juletta, I've decided. I'll take him to the *Hexe*. She'll help him."

"What do you mean, YOU'VE decided? Who was that on the phone?" Juletta's voice rang out in the silence of the kitchen.

"Hafner, he's stranded at Getchell's. The plow's in the ditch and Getchell's cut is drifted shut."

"So we're cut off too! Why didn't we go to the hospital earlier? That damn Doctor Gans. He should have known. Now what?"

"I said, I'll take him to the *Hexe*." He seemed to cringe at her voice.

Flo squealed, "Can I go too, Papa? I want to see the *Hexe* too."

"Quiet, Flo," Juletta said evenly. "Let's talk about this, Josef. He's my son too and I have a say in this. I want to try to get to the hospital. Let's take the horses and follow the highway and stop the first car going to town. They'd have to take us."

"*Nein!*" Josef's voice drowned out the radio. "What if there aren't any cars out on the highway now? Then what? I *know* it's only five miles to the Gypsy's, railroad track the last three miles. I can be there by four o'clock. For sure she'll know what to do."

"Right," Juletta retorted. "Look at me, Josef. This is what doctors are for. Maybe a hundred years ago in Germany there weren't any doctors, but we have them now." She touched his arm. "Josef, Ebbie could die."

He pulled his arm away. "Somebody has to decide and I'm the head of the house," he said. Juletta started, as if she had heard Josef's father's voice: Josef was turning into his father. She would never have married . . . Josef sat staring at the floor. Juletta knew his father would never have put up with this from *his* wife.

"Oh, I don't know what. We can't just sit. I'll have Flo and Ebbie ready by the time you're harnessed up."

"No, you're not, Juletta. You're staying here. I don't want you and Flo in the sled. Ebbie and I'll do a quick trot over there. No sense in your freezing your hinder out there too."

"Wait, who'll look after Ebbie? He's only five, Josef! What if he freezes or falls off and you don't notice?"

Josef stared at his five-buckle overshoes. "Empty the wood box and put some blankets in it. I'll put it on the sled and Ebbie can lie in it. The cover will keep the snow off his face. Do it, Juletta, don't just stand there. Right now." Josef reached for his sheepskin *pelz* on the wall, "And warm this thing up, Juletta. I'll need it."

Juletta listened to the buzz of the radio as she emptied the woodbox dirt on the floor. How could she have trusted that horse docter Gans? Now Josef was afraid and wanted to decide everything himself.

"*. . . and we'll have that new forecast in a minute after these words . . .*" Juletta put the bread on the cold floor by the door to keep it from rising, then loaded the stove with wood from the front porch. The skaters in their warm muffs continued to skate near the tall buildings that must surely hold a doctor. She lined the bottom of the box with an old quilt, two pillows and another thick blanket. She wiped her eyes and turned. "Ebbie, you're going for a sled ride. Papa will take care of you. Let's get you bundled up."

She snugged the strings on the snowsuit she'd thought was too small last year. Ebbie seemed to be shrinking. She opened the snowsuit again and removed the bag of skunk fat. She took down the crucifix and buttoned it inside his clothes.

"You're going for a ride on the sled and Mama's made a warm bed for you to sleep in." she said. She wondered how could she put her foot down now. The door opened and Josef grabbed the blankets. "I'll take these, you pack some bread and headcheese. I don't want to have to ask her for food too." The door swung back open as he left. She ran to the door and slammed it shut.

Juletta took her coat, and following Josef, carried Ebbie out the door. The wind whipped the snow into long dizzying waves low to the ground. She climbed onto the sled as Josef opened the woodbox and she laid Ebbie on the cushioned bed. Juletta kissed him and together they slowly closed the cover. She raised the cover again and stared at the pinched expression on Ebbie's blue-white face. She lowered the cover and turned to stare at Josef.

"Josef, we can't do this." The wind tore at her words. Josef looked puzzled then smiled, unsure of what she had said. "I said we can't do this," she shouted. He began to push her gently toward the edge of the sled. Juletta resisted. "No, Josef. I'm not getting off. You can't leave him in there alone. I'm going too." She threw back the cover, lifted him out and ran for the house.

Josef followed her into the bedroom. Juletta felt him at her back.

"No, you will not take him alone. You try to leave without me, you'll regret it," Juletta raged. "If he lives, I will take Ebbie and the girls and I will leave you." Josef's mouth opened but he could not speak. "Do you want to be part of the first divorce in this town? Then leave without me!" Juletta rushed past him and turned. "Then where will you belong?"

Josef stayed in the bedroom while Flo and Juletta sat stiffly on chairs in front of the open oven door. Ebbie moaned on Juletta's lap. He tried to sit straighter to ease the pain. The back of his head pushed into Juletta's chest. Juletta looked over as the bedroom door opened. Josef stared at the oven as he spoke.

"Juletta, you come too. Put Ebbie's snowsuit back on and I'll dress Flo." He spoke quietly, slowly, as if in great pain. Juletta put the flatirons on the stove, then telephoned his parents to pick up Bea and Sarah.

Josef put more straw on the oak planks. He nailed a long piece of canvas to the woodbox to make a lean-to on the sled. He brought the horse blankets and a logchain. He worked mechanically, stunned by how angry Juletta was. He'd kept what he thought was his part of the bargain, ready to make the trip through a blizzard, ready to sacrifice himself and Ebbie, so she wouldn't make a fuss. He thought of what his father would have done. He couldn't recall an angry word between his parents. Divorce. He felt maimed—as if he too had lost a hand.

Juletta followed Flo into the driving snow, hugging Ebbie to her body to keep him from blowing away. She wondered if their marriage would ever be the same. She lay Ebbie next to the woodbox and lifted Flo over the bits of manure that still clung to the edges of the planks. "This'll be the cave we hide in," she said into Flo's ear. Ebbie's face twisted in pain. "*Aufsitzen, aufsitzen,* Mama, sit me up," he cried. Juletta propped him up. She went back for the hot flat-irons then climbed in with the children. Josef looked in, his face dark against the triangle of light behind him. Their eyes did not meet.

"Giddap." The sled lurched forward into a tight turn. Prince's head and neck arched in protest at the unfamiliar rough pull on the bit. As they left the circle of buildings the canvas shuddered in the wind. Juletta shoved straw into the openings along the floor. "I don't want to go, Mama, I'm scared," Flo cried. Juletta smiled weakly in the half-light and nodded her head.

The first half mile went quickly, heading west into a northwest wind. Juletta wondered how Josef and the horses could look into the stinging biting snow. Inside her mitten, her wedding band felt loose on her cold finger. Josef turned south on the crossroad and stopped. He crouched beside the flapping canvas lean-to. His face was blasted raw and red. Snow was wedged in the space between his collar and his chin. His eyebrows were thick with snow. Ice gathered hard on his mustache. She touched his face and shouted into the wind. "Josef, you have a white spot right here. It's frostbite. Can't you turn away from the wind?"

"It'll be easier now that the wind is more behind me." Snow swirled around his face. I'll try to turn away but I need to watch the road."

"Come inside here, Josef. You can't stay out with that spot." Josef lay in the straw beside her. Ebbie sat quietly, asleep from the motion of the sled. Flo lay in the heavy blankets, one side of her face exposed. Juletta removed her heavy mittens and warmed his cheeks with her hands.

"That feels good," Josef said through his icicled mustache. She put her soft cheek next to his. "I can't stay long. I don't want the horses to stiffen up." He hesitated a moment. "You were right to come, Juletta." The wind pressed heavily on the long expanse of canvas which made the dark interior even smaller. For a moment, the wind died and it was quiet. They waited to see who would break the silence. Josef sighed. "*Nah ja*, now we just follow the road to the railroad track."

Josef returned to his team. The horses lifted their heads and he pulled the ice away from their nostrils and carefully unplugged their snow-filled ears. He snugged the straps on the horse blankets to keep the wind from lifting them off their backs. He sat on the oak planks, sheltered by the box. The sled jerked forward.

Josef's eyes picked out a pattern of weeds here, a fence line there. The wind gusted and the heavy wood box shifted behind him. He stopped the horses and came to the opening. "Juletta, I'll have to get in the box or it'll blow off. Did you feel it move?" She shook her head; her jaw was numb. He climbed into the box, turned sideways and lowered the hinged lid until it rested on his head. Only his face was exposed to biting wind. He reached one arm out to start the horses. His sheepskin *pelz* was wedged between his legs, snow blasted through the open cover. He could not distinguish between the sky and the land. He was afloat in some middle sky, the horses and sled his only anchor. The horses trotted faster, as if pushed by the quartering wind. He could be a log in the woodbox, guided only by the instincts of the horses. The cold flat disk of sun disappeared in the flying snow.

Juletta watched Ebbie's face contort in the semi-darkness. Flo complained that the wind was lifting the canvas behind her. Juletta thought of Romuald, of the Chinese, of the empty outline of the crucifix above her ironing board, of Josef invisible in the wooden box just the thickness of a board away. She thought of Stefan Ernt breathing against her bedroom door. Why couldn't he wait?

The sled suddenly capsized into the ditch, throwing Ebbie and Juletta against Flo. The woodbox, with Josef in it, stood upended in the deep snow. He was on his back, his head pushed down by the snow lodged against the cover. Josef heard the muffled cries of Ebbie and Flo. In the tight space, he turned his body around, cursing the length of his greatcoat. He pushed against the woodbox cover. It opened and he fell flat on his face. A gust of wind drove icy pellets of snow up his nostrils. He struggled to his feet, fell again, then righted himself. Dan was up to his belly in the ditch. Prince lay on his side partially propped up by Dan's broad back under him. Josef ran around the horses, past their white-rimmed eyes. He loosened Prince's traces from the doubletree to keep him from tangling the harness. Juletta climbed out.

"Just a minute Flo," Juletta said. "No, you can't come out. The wind will blow you away." She looked at the sled and the team.

"Josef," she shouted.

He pointed up the road. "See for yourself. That line of grass along the road is all the horses can see. Stay under the canvas and keep the kids quiet. Hand me that shovel from in there."

Josef shoveled the snow from around Prince's legs and led him to the back of the sled. The horses were old and experienced and not quick to panic, though Prince eyed the heaving canvas. His hands numb on the shovel handle, Josef freed Dan who emerged from the ditch a ghost horse, dusted all over with a fine powder of snow. Josef grabbed the log chain and hitched the horses to the back of the sled. "Hold on tight, we're going backwards now." Prince heaved into the load, "Not yet, god damn it. Whoa, Prince." The rear skids of the sled had swiveled, wedging into the snow behind them.

"Juletta, I can't do this alone. You lead Prince while I jam the shovel next to the runner to keep it from twisting." Juletta's long coat swirled out in the wind. Josef yelled. "No, no. Approach him from the front. He's already spooked." Juletta made the half circle and took the halter.

Josef shouted again, over the howl of the storm. "When I say so, lead them to the center of the road. Giddap, Prince. That's it, Dan. Lean into it." The sled jerked and the rear skid inched past Josef's shovel. The front skid straightened when it reached the road. Josef smiled as he helped Juletta get back under the canvas.

Walking beside the horses, Josef hid behind their heavy bodies for protection from the wind. The woodbox didn't move now, lashed to the sled with the log chain. Under the canvas, Juletta and Flo thrashed their legs and hugged the flat irons to keep warm. Ebbie was warm under the stack of blankets.

Without warning, the road rose under Josef's leaden feet. "It's the track," he yelled, "we're getting closer, Juletta."

Josef turned the sled into the space between the tracks. The roadbed stood high above the prairie. Its deep ditches were nearly full of snow. As the horses turned, the wind struck them even harder than before, but they seemed pleased with the definite edges of the railroad bed. They increased their pace at Josef's hoarse cries. Soon a house rose up out of the swirling snow. Josef ran to their heads and led the horses to the side of the house out of the wind.

"Anybody in there?" Josef's heavy leather choppers pounded the twisted door. "HEY, anybody in there?" A stricken look crossed his frosted face. He screamed toward the sled, "Juletta, JULETTA. There's no one here!" He stepped back to stare at the crumbling chimney. then felt the peeling door with his bare hand. The snow under his frozen feet squealed as he lumbered toward the triangle of the canvas. Juletta's back was to him. She had lifted the blankets and opened Ebbie's clothes. She whirled to look over her shoulder.

"It's worse, Josef, look at it now." She jerked him under the canvas. "See how much it's swollen." Her voice rose. "You and your dumb superstitions. But it's my fault, isn't it? I've been so stupid all these years. You should've married that little Beatrice of yours, just left me out of this . . ."

"Juletta," Josef's voice hissed in the quiet of the sled. "What is *wrong* with you? For Christ's sake, the children can hear. . ."

"What? What?" Juletta's voice rose again. "Our son is dying. We're stuck in the middle of a blizzard. In front of some damn Gypsy's house. And you're worried what the children will think? *Bista ganz verrückt?* I can't be angry about this?" She flung her arm out and shoved Josef out of her way. She ran to the door and gave it a tremendous shove. The door gave way, throwing Juletta into the center of the small dark room.

"Can I help you?" came a quiet voice from the floor. Juletta stared wildly about her. The voice came from a pile of blankets near the stove. "I have nothing of value." In the light from the open door, the dark blankets shifted and a face peered out of a woolen scarf. "Please close the door."

Juletta rose then stumbled over the folds of her coat. She closed the door. The light from the heavily curtained window revealed only the outlines of the room, a stove, a sink, a table, another door.

"Are you the Gypsy?" Juletta's voice cracked.

"No, I am not." A gust of wind whistled in the stovepipe. The woman spoke again. "I am called the Gypsy."

"What I mean is, do you claim to heal people? My son, he has . . . there's a lump down here and it's bulging out."

"You came to me for help?" The pile of blankets moved to reveal the shape of the woman's head. "I can't travel far."

"But he's here, I mean, he's outside in the sled."

"You brought a child in this wind?" She struggled to prop herself on her elbows. "And you left him outside? Bring him inside."

Juletta turned to see Josef open the door. "Josef, she's here. Quick, bring him in." She followed Josef through the cascade of snow drifting down the sloping roof. Ebbie cried out when Josef moved him, whimpering into the heavy wool coat.

Flo squinted at the bright light. "*Wo ist dann die Hexe?* Where is she?" Juletta clamped her hand over Flo's mouth.

"Shhh! Don't say that word. Please, please don't say it."

She followed Josef into the house. Josef hesitated, turning from side to side. The room went dark as Juletta closed the door.

"Put him on the table. Your name is?"

"Josef."

"Yoo-seff," she repeated. "And?"

"Juletta."

"Chew-letta." She slumped back under the heavy cover and stared at the dark ceiling. "Chew-letta," she repeated. There was a silence. "I am Roma," she said finally.

"And my son's name is Eberhard and this is Florence and can't we start now, for God's sake? Is there a light?"

"Of course, there's a lamp by the sink. Don't open the curtain, the wind comes right through the glass. And Yoo-seff, there's wood through that door. I keep dry wood." She paused. "I believe in that."

Juletta saw the outline of the lamp. She felt the windowsill for matches then spotted a tin matchbox hanging on the wall. The lamp flickered and smoked as the light from the kerosene lamp threw deep shadows on the wall. Ebbie saw his mother wavering in the light and cried out, "*Aufsitzen*, Mama." Juletta propped him against the wall. Josef poked the fire and the flame spurted. The mountain of blankets toppled and the woman stood slowly. She was dressed to go directly into the storm. Her heavy leather boots creaked as she walked. She took off her scarf and smoothed the thick hair that flowed down her back.

"Chewletta, bring the lamp, let's take a look." Her smooth face shone in the light; her dark eyes looked into Juletta's face. She smiled at Ebbie and her fingers flew over his clothing, undoing the ties and buttons. She hesitated a moment. She turned and looked at them, each in turn, then took the crucifix from his chest.

"He'll have to stand now, I can't tell the size while he's sitting." The lump was larger than a turkey egg. She looked at them.

"Why didn't you come earlier? This is serious."

Both Josef and Juletta answered at once, then stopped.

"I see. There was some disagreement. Cover him while I warm my hands." Her boots creaked across the floor. She opened the stove door and held her hands directly above the small flame.

"Put in more wood, Yoo-seff. It's cold out here."

She returned to the table.

"Hold his shoulder, this may hurt."

"Wait, what are you going to do? What do you know about this?"

"Juletta!" Josef warned. "You have to believe or it won't work."

"No, Yoo-seff, she needn't believe in this. This is not a matter for the mind. Part of the gut has pushed through the boy's muscle here. It has to pushed back gently, gently. This is bad but I have seen worse." She reached forward then covered him again.

"All this talk and my hands are cold again." She strode quickly to the stove and put her hands over the building flames.

"Chewletta, the shoulders, Yoo-seff, hold his feet." Her strong white hands gently kneaded the outer edges of the sloping lump.

Ebbie whimpered but watched with fearful eyes. Slowly the lump was reduced to the size of a pullet egg. Finally, the skin lay flat.

Juletta stared into the woman's face. "Is that it, is that all? Could I have done that?"

"Could you have done that?" She looked at Juletta. "I don't know. I know the body and the spirit and how they work together, but I cannot *heal* this. We'll wrap him tight so the lump won't come out. The boy needs a hospital and a doctor with a knife. He needs them soon, tomorrow or the next day. At noon the train stops four miles west of here to drop the mail at Regal. You can stay here tonight. If you take the train, you will be at the hospital by evening."

Ebbie lay asleep under the blankets Juletta had brought from the sled. Flo sat near the roaring stove that the Gypsy had fed to a dull red glow. Juletta sat stiffly in a straight-backed chair and watched the woman return with a cooking pot filled with snow from beside the door. The clump of the Gypsy's boots sounded on the cellar steps. Juletta took off her mitten and her ring clattered to the floor. She reached quickly to pick it up and return it to her finger. The Gypsy returned with an oak basket filled with potatoes and onions and a rough slab of dried meat. Josef's bread and headcheese lay on the rough table. In a more familiar house, Juletta's hands would have itched to help. The knot in her shoulders had loosened. She watched Ebbie sleep, grateful that the Gypsy could do that much for him. She was incapable of the easy smile that Josef flashed at the Gypsy when he knew that she could help Ebbie. To give in to all this would be to draw her further from the modern life she had known at the Erntses' warm and comfortable house.

She paced to the window and back, then went outside into the swirling, roaring whiteout. Joseph had unhitched the horses and had taken them into the barn. Chickens scratched quietly in the hay-filled barn. Josef had spread oats from a sack and was feeding the horses the musty hay. The door opened and Juletta walked through the bright opening. He smiled at her and bent his back to his work. They both waited in the hay-shrouded silence.

"*Was kann Ich dir sagen?*" Juletta said. "What can I say, Josef? You'll hold it against me, even if you never say anything."

Josef shrugged under his heavy coat and continued to rub the horses' legs with a dry gunny sack.

She looked down at the chickens. "Maybe the Gypsy could hypnotize me so I wouldn't care. I don't know if I can live like this."

"Like what?"

"Like I don't count for anything. You have all these ideas I can't believe in, don't want to believe in, ideas I don't even know you have until suddenly you're deciding things for all of us, even putting our lives in danger, bulling ahead like I'm not even here. I want to be with you, Josef, but you're living in the past. We can't go back a hundred years to some hut in a German forest." She looked at the chickens again. "The Gypsy could never hypnotize me so I wouldn't care."

Josef shook his head and took her into his arms. "It will be better." He kissed her and stroked the tears from her eyes. "I promise you." She willed her body to relax, to fill only the space alloted to her. She did not know if it would be better. They stood in the silence of the barn, separated only by their heavy coats and the faint but unmistakable smell of skunk fat.

Mrs. Cabot and Mrs. Abernathy

School looks easy after a summer of making hay, taking care of the chickens, the pigs, and the cows, and sweating in the potato patch behind the busch. By the time Uncle Willem's threshing machine trundles out of our yard, summer feels like it's over and good riddance. On August 15th, the feast of the Assumption of the Blessed Virgin into Heaven, a Church holiday when Catholics can't work, we drive the forty miles to St. Cloud to shop for school and ride the elevator in the medical building. The town is packed with people buying school supplies and practicing their city driving. After a day of tramping through the crowds, shopping for shoes, shirts and school supplies, we're ready to meet my father at the Über Eck bar by the courthouse where the air is thick with the sound of German, the smell of roast beef, sausage, sauerkraut, stale beer and snuff.

On Sunday afternoon, Uncle Jerome comes over with eleven of his thirteen children, my favorite set of cousins. We show them our school stuff and come back downstairs where Uncle Jerome says he has news for us. He's in our hot kitchen, his flannel shirt buttoned up to the bulging folds of his neck, his thick hands folded over his beer belly, a resigned look on his face. "*Ja,* you kits," he starts, "you know your old teacher Mrs. Timlich died . . . you don't find teachers like Aegidia Timlich nowadace." He stops, schnappering for breath after all these words. He glances out the window, shakes his head and continues.

"We offered fifty dollars at the county office. *Nichts.* Fifty dollars a month! What for a world do we lif in, anywace? We offered fifty-five.

Chust the one teacher wants it. Zo," he shakes his head again then blurts out, "we're going to haf a *Protestant* for a teacher at Boxelder School."

I'd seen Protestants before. Sitting below the sign flashing ON AND OFF-SALE LIQUOR, I'd watch them come into Meinulph's Saloon. Some of them wear Sunday clothes, others, railroad overalls. They drive in from Kandiyohi County, a Protestant place that always votes itself dry. They have their lists of liquor in hand: gin, scotch, vodka, and rum, hard stuff we never drink in Stearns County. They don't speak our language but something called Scandahoovian.

Old bald Meinulph, his back so humped he has to crick his neck to look at you, runs a heavy hand across his head with a surprised look on his face. Like he'd gone bald overnight. Leaning on his cane, he takes the orders and Toby, his no-good grandson, brings up the bottles from the open cases in the cellar. Meinulph puts the bottles in boxes as Toby brings full cases to the back door. The Protestants lick their lead pencils and cross off words on the crumpled pieces of paper in the palms of their hands. They count out wads of money, wrinkled money they gather from their friends and neighbors for the liquor run. It's this business that keeps our cattle trucker, Werner Schmolz, busy, bringing Meinulph liquor by the truckload on his return trip from the stockyards. It's odd, these grown men bragging about sneaking bottles back home, right under their wives' noses. I keep thinking, why don't the men vote wet too?

No Protestants live near us, but driving to Paynesville, a large town with four different churches, my father points out a run-down farm with shabby buildings and unditched fields half-covered with water and says: "Now there's a Protestant farm." A wave of pity sweeps over us.

On the first day of school, I am a little nervous about my first face-to-face contact with a Protestant. We all stare at the beat-up little Protestant trailer house Uncle Jerome let her park next to the school for free. I am relieved when I see Mrs. Cabot smiling on the steps of the school, twirling the hand bell in her hand. She is short, heavy set, with gray hair and glasses that flash in the sun. Mrs. Cabot has arranged the single room by grades, our names written in boxes chalked on the blackboard: four rows of desks on runners for the eight grades. There are thirty of us. She smiles and writes her name in the single box at the top of the blackboard in her perfect Palmer handwriting. She smiles again as she turns to call the roll. When my cousin Alvis, who is sitting in the front seat closest to her, answers, "here," she gives him a hard look.

"Alois" she says, pronouncing the "o" like an "o" instead of a "v" like everyone else does. The folds of her neck wobble, "Alvis, what do you have in your mouth? Is that licorice?"

"No, teacher." Alvis opens his mouth wide to prove it. What she thinks is licorice is the rot in Alvis's teeth. Each of his teeth is rotted from both sides, so that all you can see are little points, like the tips of sharp pencils. He looks like those wild men with the filed teeth in the Maryknoll mission magazine. Alvis's family doesn't eat butter: they eat syrup by the gallon. Alvis and his five brothers and sisters all carry their lunch to school in empty syrup pails. Mrs. Cabot is so shocked at his teeth, she can hardly stop looking at him. She walks past Alvis's desk to mine and tells me to stand. She asks me to open my mouth. She puts her hand on my jaw to turn my face toward the window. Her big bosoms push against me and the wrinkled skin of her forearm brushing against mine feels like ragged paper. She wears perfume, though she's far from young. She counts eight black teeth. Mrs. Cabot looks at us for a long time then stares out of the window, not saying a word.

She finds out almost no one in the school owns a toothbrush. When Alvis says he thought his mother had one he could use, Mrs. Cabot tells us that each of us has to have his own toothbrush, no sharing, and she wants us to bring them to school, all on the same day. Our parents complain, but what can they do—she is the teacher.

When we get the toothbrushes, we find we don't have time to use them. We have cattle and hogs to feed, babies to care for in the morning. So she gets the idea of taking morning roll call by having us answer yes or no, according to whether we'd brushed our teeth.

The next morning, she takes out her red roll call book and begins with the eighth graders. My cousin, Gregor, who already does most of the milking and often drives to school with Uncle Willem's pickup, answers with a deep: "Yes."

"Good, Gregor. And now, Rosalie, did you brush your teeth?"

"Yes, teacher."

The room is silent. We know they haven't brushed their teeth. No one says a word because no one wants to make a fuss. Mrs. Cabot continues down the list. It's yes, yes, yes, right down to my sister Rita in the first grade, who can't pronounce her s's.

"Yeth. Yeth, I did brush my teeth, teacher."

Suddenly the road to hell seems paved with rotting teeth. We all know we'll have to confess this sin to Father Reiter. Being a Protestant, Mrs. Cabot doesn't know anything about that.

So every morning at roll call we lie, committing venial sins that, inevitably, become mortal sins. When you confess a sin, you have to intend never to commit it again or it becomes a mortal sin. A bad confession becomes a worse sin if you fail to own up to it the next time. If you die in a state of mortal sin, that bad confession can send you straight to the jaws of hell. We could be looking at an eternity of hell thinking: God, if only I'd brushed my teeth.

She tells us we need a check-up from the dentist too. So she makes up a dental card and copies it on the jelly hectograph, insisting a dentist has to sign them and that we turn them in.

A Dr. Davis, the undertaker's brother, is found to be the nearest dentist. Our parents ring up Central to make appointments for all of us. When we learn that he is a Protestant too, we do not dismiss this as a mere coincidence. What is this ungodly interest Protestants have in teeth? We think they have more important things to worry about, like their immortal souls, and the error of their ways.

When the day of our appointment comes, we drive by Meinulph's Saloon with its usual pack of strangers loading liquor into cars and then past the run-down farm to far-off Paynesville, that Protestant town. Up to now our father had taken care of our teeth with a pair of dental pliers he bought from Kellner's Grocery next to the saloon. We wonder if he'll be like the other Protestants we know so far, maybe a run-down office and a rack of pliers . . . a bottle of gin?

We are surprised to find a waiting room with clean white walls and those wavy glass block windows you can't really see anything through, just squiggly shapes, like at the bottom of a stock tank. I assume later that Dr. Davis doesn't want witnesses to the torture we suffer. We stand by the slippery chairs in the waiting room and stare at the table telephone with numbers in a round dial. We have the wall-mounted kind that rings two long and one short.

My sister Laura pokes me in the ribs. I turn angrily to look at her. She gives me a look and jerks her head toward a spot above the telephone. On the wall in a gold frame is a certificate with red ink and a gold seal, saying that Dr. Davis is a Thirty-Third Degree Mason. We've heard about the Masons in catechism class, their secret handshakes, the hocus pocus making fun of the Mass. We stand there open-mouthed, wondering what will happen next.

A door swings open and Dr. Davis's nurse waltzes in with the most beautiful hair, black with a few long strands of gray, all smooth and shiny above her perfect white uniform. Her name, Mrs. Abernathy, is printed in blue letters on a shiny piece of plastic. She doesn't look like anybody from our side; by the time a woman has any gray hair, she usually has six to twelve children and years of home cooking behind her. Not Mrs. Abernathy. Her waist, cinched in with a narrow white belt, is as tiny as some fifteen-year-old *Mädel*'s.

"What beautiful children." she warbles. We all turn, looking behind us to see who had come in.

"No, I mean you." She kneels down in front of my little sister, who looks okay, I guess, if she's combed the *fratzen* out of her hair. Mrs. Abernathy checks the piece of paper in her hand. Her perfume wafts by us. "You must be Rita." I can only think of the Protestants in Meinulph's saloon and their lists. Rita's eyes light up like she's been handed an ice cream cone.

"Yeth, I am. Are you a Prothethant?"

Mrs. Abernathy pauses just a second then smiles. She shows her perfect teeth, her lips outlined with hot red lipstick.

"Yes, I am, Rita. How *ever* did you guess?"

She smiles, reading the rest of our names off the paper. In her softest, kindest voice she half-breathes half-whispers, to - have - a - seat and make - your - selves - com - fort - able. She leaves and we look at each other with raised eyebrows. She's so nice it makes us nervous. Suddenly this feels like the waiting room to hell or like we're Hansel and Gretel with a big surprise in store for us. We stare at the ceiling lights which are that long kind, cool looking like the nurse. We wait our turn, the four of us, squirming on the shiny surface of the chairs, fogging over the silvery metal of the armrests with our horrible Catholic breath, until Doctor Davis comes out.

Dr. Davis must be close to eighty, with a short white crew-cut of thick hair. And hands that shake. Someone said his hand slipped last month and he drilled into the tongue of one of the men from town. We don't know if the man was Catholic.

With all the enthusiasm of a convict facing the rope, I follow Dr. Davis into the office and slide onto the dentist's chair. Dr. Davis wears thick glasses, and over them a heavy gray dental visor and over it, a third small glass that extends almost into my face. As I look into all these lenses, his eyes look miles away, his breath as short as if he'd just walked all those miles. As he goes by me, I catch a whiff of perfume. Dr. Davis wears a scent, like the perfume Mrs. Cabot and Mrs. Abernathy wear. Where do they teach this, I wonder, and what does it mean?

Dr. Davis pumps up the dentist chair as fast as he can, as if he can't wait to see what pain he can inflict. He scratches at my teeth with a silver pick, poking at exposed nerves with what feels like a hot wire. He shakes his head sadly, like Uncle Jerome in our hot kitchen. I think I detect a small smile on his lips. He turns toward a cabinet of shiny drawers and returns with a long pointy syringe like we use to vaccinate cattle. He drives the skinny point into my gums, stopping only as the needle bumps my rotting teeth. He pushes on the plunger like he's dynamiting tree stumps. Three seconds later he jabs at my gums with a pick.

"YOU FEEL THAT?" he bellows, his fist and the long pick still in my mouth.

"Ahhnnnnnn-uh," I reply, nodding yes.

He holds the syringe up to the long cool lights, and gives me another jolt to the gums. On the other side of the wavy glass, I can see the shadowy forms of people walking Main Street. There is no use yelling. It is a Protestant town.

"FEEL THAT?"

Of course I can, but my gums will burst if he gives me another shot. "NUH-uhnnnn." I shake my head no, lying to a Protestant about my teeth again. He swings a tray of picks and drill bits in front of my face. I stare at the jumble of equipment. On my left, there's a contraption that ends in a drill, driven by a heavy cord strung through pullies. He loads a drill bit into the drill and begins to work. The green fabric covering the cord is frayed in places and the loose ends of the fabric whirl through the pullies like little green flags urging him on. The whine of the drill rises and falls in that small room like the far-off voices of the damned.

"Wider, open wider."

My mouths is open as wide as it goes. My lips ache from being stretched so tight.

"AUF-MACHEN!," he shouts, "OPEN UP."

He's using his school German on me, as if I can't understand him. I think he's getting even with me for something, maybe because we belong to the One True Church.

"AUF-MACHEN, GOD DAMN IT."

Mrs. Abernathy glides in and stands by my elbow. Her soft hand touches mine. She moves so I can see her eyes and she smiles.

"Are you all right?" she asks. "This is always difficult, isn't it? Be brave." She turns to Dr. Davis. "Let's allow the Novocain to take hold, Doctor. It's their first time, so be gentle."

She smiles her finest whitest smile and I know she's on my side. She turns, her arms raised slightly, as if demonstrating her tiny waist, and leaves the room. Dr. Davis looks over his shoulder at her then turns back to me.

"And keep it open, damn it," he hisses under his breath.

He pushes down on the drill, his knee coming up to the seat of the chair for leverage. The smell of decayed teeth rises like the odor of brimstone. I try to adjust what I know about Protestants to somehow include Mrs. Abernathy. I think back to how Sister Mary Benedict explained about Moses and John the Baptist and other good people who lived before Jesus. They were Catholics but they didn't know it. Mrs. Abernathy has to be one of us.

At this point I come to a decision. I'll show Dr. Davis what stern stuff Catholics are made of. He won't hear me griping or see me wince. I won't give him the satisfaction. I'd be the Catholic who could look a Mason in the eye and not blink.

"Wider," he says, "WIDER."

He puts little pieces of metal around maybe three teeth at a time, I can't tell, and giant wads of cotton, and more fingers. I know he'd throw in a pipe wrench and a hog trough too, if there were room. But not a peep from me. He may as well be working on a corpse.

A shadowy figure hesitates on the other side of the wavy glass. I will not cry out. The figure moves on. I have the example of saints and martyrs to live up to. If St. Laurence, the first saint to undergo the torture of the grill, could look up and tell his torturers that he was done on one side and to turn him over—then I could take the heat too.

"AUF-MACHEN. Wider. Wider." Dr. Davis's shaking hand holds a drill. He reaches into my mouth, into the small unoccupied space.

My tongue curls up and away from the tool. He grunts as his foot searches for the foot pedal. He won't hear a peep out of me. If these fillings never come out, it's because they're rooted in my Catholic soul.

Old Schuler

In a single room, where gray light filters through ice-covered windows, a bed is piled high with cloth blankets and lush fur pelts: mink, beaver, a red fox, racoon, more mink. Two hands gently, gently now, tug at a quilt. A long red nose, anchored in sallow wrinkled flesh, twitches. Ripples spread outward across the bony face. Eyeballs under wrinkled lids dart from side to side under a crudely-stitched fur hat cocked at eyebrow level.

Schuler is dreaming. A stone statue of the Good Shepherd comes to life, strides past cemetery pines, down gravel roads, back to the old cemetery at Stony Creek. He dreams of an open grave. A coffin is lifted on stony shoulders, long strides move down a path barely visible, past scattered islands of rustling milkweed pods, back through cemetery pines, under the castiron arch that reads *Ruhet in Frieden.* The Gothic letters S-C-H, crudely carved, float like a mirage over the box. He strains forward to read his name, dry tongue scraping dry cracked lips. He has died! It has been easy. He strains further, opens his eyes wider, . . . and wakes. His dry eyes creak open in the half-darkness of the gray light. No, he is still alive. A dream!

Thirst overwhelms every other sensation. Schuler holds his tongue immobile in his mouth, careful that it not snap. He moves swiftly from the bed, furs slipping noiselessly to the dirt-encrusted floor. His strong smooth hands grasp the handle of the cistern pump. He hears the dry leathers of the pump wheeze in the cavern below the floor. The weight of the water in the pipe increases. He pumps faster, recklessly, his elbow flailing outward until the first silver drops break across the lip of the spout. He bends, turns his head and the water pours over his face and into his mouth. His throat contracts above the cavern of his shrunken stomach. He pumps furiously, gulping, gasping, half-drowning, the water sieving through every dusty cell—he is alive.

A high Arctic wind knifes across prairie fields toward groaning oaks, driving ahead of it an onslaught of snow, a swarm of flying needles that slash at the exposed eyes of the dark bundle mining rock-hard shards of flesh from a mound of frozen animal carcasses. In the dying light, his axe slices through frozen flesh into hard bone. Nearby, row upon row of wire cages heave with the frenzied bodies of sleek mink, driven nearly-mad by four days of hunger. Their flinty eyes watch greedily for the meat he will bring. Schuler straightens a little, irritably raising the heavy leather mitten to swipe at the drop of water that clings to the end of his red nose, a drop that suddenly threatens his fever-weakened balance. He sees the drop pitching him face forward, one more corpse on a snow-drifted pile of corpses.

He bends in search of the meat saw. A gust of snow infiltrates a gap at his collar. At his back, he feels the tug of the line that moors him to his house. His eyes scan the snow; the meat-saw has disappeared. He kneels on one knee, bracing his body against the upright axe. With his free hand, he sweeps the ground for the oblong shape of the saw. His hand, bound in heavy leather, claws at the snow. He steadies himself on the axehandle and pushes himself up from his knees. The image of an arthritic bishop, raising himself with his golden crozier at Confirmation, intrudes on his thoughts. *Bitt' für uns, bitt' für uns,* he mumbles. Pray for us, now and in the hour of our death.

He shakes his head. The task at hand, he bends to it now. But how not to think of death, blinded by the snow, sawing off protruding parts of corpses wherever his unsteady feet gain purchase on the slippery surfaces? Fool! Take the easy road, worry about tomorrow tomorrow.

Frozen blood flies from the biting edge of the saw like sawdust. The hairy hide of a cow's leg, he makes a game of it: a sow's ear, a horse's ass. He piles the rock-hard pieces into a zinc tub. He will drag the parts to his house, thaw them overnight, portion out the pieces to fit through the small doors of the cages. He weeps, knowing death will not come easily.

Taking Stock

We've got the pinkeye, all ten of us kids. We sit around the house with the shades pulled, knirpsing quietly in the dark like chickens when the winter night lasts sixteen hours. We have strict orders not to look out, but a peddler comes selling fire extinguishers from farm to farm. Gregor can't resist raising the corner of the shade to see him showing my father how to put out a pan of flaming kerosene with a blast from the red tube. Less than a month later, Gregor is complaining about his eyes so much that the doctor says he needs glasses. My parents curse the peddler for the extra expense, but, *was muss muss,* and they pay.

After the pink-eye we get the chicken pox, all ten of us. It's still winter. My mother has used up every distraction she can think of, so she says we all need to learn tatting, lacemaking, even us two boys. My older sisters, Anna and Barbara, can already do rings, picots, and slip joins. My mother starts them on reversing work and locking joins so they can make small doilies. The rest of us, including us two lummoxes, begin with the simplest double stitch and chain. After a day or two, I can do them well enough to tat a straight line of rings to lace a handkerchief. My left hand stiffens up like an old lady's as I make the loop for the shuttle to pass through for the double stitch. But it's better than staring at the radio, where three or four hours of Whoopee John's polkas and schottisches a day are more than enough.

My mother shows us a handkerchief she laced when she was little—so tight, straight and even. Amazing, how you can take a straight piece of cotton thread and make beautiful rings spin out from the tatting shuttle. Before long, Gregor and I are racing to see who can make the longest chain, something my mother can see no use for, but at least we're not fighting. Gregor and I are just waiting to get away from the cooking, the mending, the dishwashing and our sisters; a world we know is way too small for us.

When we're well enough to go back to work and school, I think I'll never tat again. But at the end of January, despite the little bags of *shtink-katz fett*, skunk fat, pinned to our undershirts, we all come down with the flu, the achy joints and sore throat kind. We had just missed St. Blaise Day, February 2nd, by a few days, when old Father Reiter would have blessed our throats with two sweet-smelling beeswax candles held in a V, our coats open for the smooth wax to brush against our necks, to prevent just this kind of problem. To ease our throats, we drink hot honey water. The sound of spoons ringing out against so many cups fills the house. This is during the polio so we go to Melrose for polio shots too, after which something changes, so Gregor and I don't want go back to tatting anymore. We want to get away from the house altogether, but we're still sick.

My mother sighs and gets out her long shiny Stricknadeln and tries to teach us how to knit. After a day or two of half-hearted tries, Gregor and I will have no more of it. Anna has to grab the needles before we put each other's eyes out.

About this time the steer market is topping out with prices at record highs. My father decides to ship half our steers to catch the peak of the market. He calls Werner Schmolz, our trucker, to arrange the shipping to South St. Paul later in the week. Werner suggests a night of rabbit hunting in the meantime. We make a show of being well, so we can go along. Our mother sees through it but gives in.

It's a cloudy night, with a few patches of clear to show a three-quarter moon, when we all gather around the '49 Hudson. We call it the new car, even though it's five years old and has a big gash in the hood where my father took an axe to it when it wouldn't start for the thirtieth day in a row. We're taking the Hudson because it's big and has a side-mounted spotlight we can use for shining rabbits. The engine of Werner's '38 Olds ticks quietly as it cools down after the trip from town, all the while he's bragging how good a shot he is.

In a few minutes we're loaded into the big bench seats, my father driving, Werner and Reiner, our hired man, and Romuald, my uncle Magnus's hired man, sitting next to the doors, their shotgun barrels sticking out of the open windows. My brother and I are sitting in the middle, me between Werner and my father, Gregor in the back because he's eleven and I'm only nine. Both of us boys are avoiding the shiny wooden shotgun stocks that dig into our ribs as the shooters shift in the awkward space.

We've had only a few feet of snow this winter and a big January thaw, so clumps of dirt from last fall's plowing are showing everywhere. It's perfect for spotting the winter-white jackrabbits as we drive slowly down the frozen gravel roads. My father's right hand is on the wheel, his left sweeps the fields with the spotlight. His shotgun is on the seat next to his door, sticking almost straight up out of his open window.

We're hardly out of sight of the busch that surrounds our yard when the first jack comes bounding toward the headlights from the right. His long ears fly up as he lands and lie flat along his back as he rises. Werner yells, "Fer Chrissake, Willem, stop. Don't you see him?" My father hits the brakes. My father and Romuald sitting behind him, both get off a shot, just as the jack turns. I suspect my father didn't have time enough to aim, driving and all. The noise of the two blasts and the smell of the powder fill the car and leave our ears ringing like a church steeple.

By now the heater is blasting streams of hot air while cold air comes in through the open windows. We're packed in so tight, we have to struggle to loosen our heavy coats. Werner is able to get at the pint he stashes in his coat pocket and shoves it into his big graying beard, then passes it over my head just as Romuald yells and fires out his window at another rabbit that seems to come out of nowhere. This jackrabbit tumbles forward and rolls a few feet, so by the time my father gets the spotlight on him, he's dead. I run out to pick him up and throw him on the gunny sacks in the trunk for Romuald, who skins jacks and sells the pelts to add a few dollars to the low wages Uncle Magnus pays him. Romuald is working harder now for the same money, because Magnus has added fifty head of young stock, thinking the steer market will last forever.

After an hour and a half we've got seven jacks. Our ears are ringing, our clothes stink of gunpowder that overpowers even the smell of *shtinkkatz fett.* Werner is nervously chewing snuff, fuming that he hasn't gotten off even one good shot. He *shpuks* snuff juice out the front window, while Reiner in back complains the juice is fouling his shotgun. Werner passes the bottle and swears we won't quit until he gets a jack. We make another sweep by Schuler's place and then past my grandfather's woodlot. We all see the movement to the right of the headlights and yell for my father to stop. He does, raking the car across the road toward the ditch so Werner can get off a shot, just as the rabbit crosses the road. Through the roar and the blue smoke, the jack does not lose a step.

"Verdammt noch a mal, I musta got that son-of-a-bitch." Werner yells. "*Wo ist er dann?* Where'd he go, Willem?" he asks as my father stops at the spot where the jack crossed the road. Werner leaps out and we follow, the guns pointing down for the first time. Werner tells Gregor, whose turn it is, to look near the ditch right next to the road. Gregor stiefels through the deep snow and turns into the light, raising his arms like there's nothing out there. *The light is shining off his glasses,* so what do they expect?

"*Guck doch,* Gregor!" Werner yells at him and "See, I hit the bastard," he yells at us, pointing to a single drop of blood on the hump of the road. My brother makes another zigzag try and comes back empty-handed. I can see Werner is tempted to go after it himself, but I think he's afraid he'd founder in the ditch like a horse in deep snow, he's so big. He looks at me.

"Lucas, think you can find him?"

I nod and shift the spotlight a bit and slog across the ditch to the plowed field. I can hardly see my brother's boot tracks, much less the track of a fast-moving jack hitting frozen ground every fifteen feet. I angle back and forth along the light from the spotlight, until by accident I come across a few drops of blood on some snow but by now I've come to the end of the cone of light.

Just then the moon breaks through the clouds, lighting a south-facing slope where all the snow has melted. In the middle of the black dirt I see a white spot that has to be the rabbit. I leave the spotlight and go down the bank through the dark, my feet catching in the dry bromus grass. I cross the frozen crick to head up the hill toward the rabbit. It's lying by a tiny bit of blood near its head that close up looks red until the moon goes under a cloud. Then it turns black as the night. Through my mittens, I feel the heat of the rabbit's foot, this foot not lucky for this rabbit.

I'm not tall enough to carry the long jack in one hand and I don't want to drag it with its head and soft ears bumping over the clumps of dirt; so I carry it in my arms, holding it away from my coat. Suddenly I feel like I'm bringing Werner a gift in my outstretched arms, which it is in a way, him so worried about not getting anything so far. The moon is gone and I'm headed back to the cone of spotlight which is tripping over the rough plowed field looking for me. I'm tripping, too, over the clumps in the darkness toward it. The sound of hallohing rings out as the light from the headlights flickers off and on again as someone steps in and out of the path of light.

It's Werner, pacing in front of the headlights, who spots me. He lets out a yell saying he knew he'd gotten off a good shot. Once the jack is lying on the road in front of the headlights, anybody can see only a few pellets grazed its head, one going through the eye and into, I think, the brain. Werner's luck is better than the jack's but I don't say anything.

Werner looks me straight in the face and tells me what a good hunter I am. He turns to my dad and asks if it'd be all right with him if I went with the load of steers to South Saint Paul as a reward. Gregor, being older and not having gone, gives me a dirty look. This is something I'd begged Werner for many times but he'd always said no. Now he says to my father that he'd be sure nothing happened to me, provided of course that it was okay with my mother. My father slowly agrees, knowing how bad I want to go. My father's only argument had been that Werner wouldn't want me along. I look over at Gregor and for once I've got something over him. I don't care how often he gets to be Joe Louis and I have to be Jersey Joe Walcott and get knocked out all the time as we box on the double bed we share. Nobody's ever heard of a champ wearing glasses.

I make sure I stop *schnooffling* and I swallow my coughs when there's anyone around, because I know this is my big chance to go to the Cities. My mother looks at me the way she does when she's ready to say no. I know sometimes she thinks Werner is a *shtoffel.* But then she surprises me by agreeing I can go. She tells me to be careful and stay out of the way.

About eight o'clock, Werner pulls up under the polelight in our yard. We load the fifteen heaviest steers, the rest being too light to be sold as anything but stockers and feeders. We load them without too much trouble, but still a lot of swearing from Werner as usual. Werner and his brother Lodder, who is also a trucker, are the only truckers I know. Both of them swear so much I think that, because of their jobs, it isn't a sin for truckers to swear. They swear in both English and High German, in

Preissich, my parents' dialect as well as in Plattdeutsch, our neighbor's dialect, some words I can't even guess at the meaning. Usually they swear in just one language at a time, unless they are loading my Uncle Jerome's sheep. Then they mix all the words together, calling the sheep every dirty word possible. Still the sheep won't go up the chute by themselves. They have to carry them up the chute by the back wool, which makes sheep a lot smarter than cattle or hogs, who willingly go to their deaths. But then you can't really tell sheep anything they haven't thought of themselves in their pointy little heads, which for the most part must be pretty empty.

With Gregor just standing there still not believing I'm going, Werner and I leave our farm, the load of steers bawling in the back of the green International truck. I've got my red and blue Lone Ranger wallet with a green dollar tucked in the secret pocket I *finally* have a use for; though my father tells me to keep the wallet in my front pocket anyway, just like at the county fair. The huge engine is roaring away just feet from where I sit high on Werner's fat sheep-skin *pelz* so I can see out of the window. The smell of oil drifts through the leaky fire wall, enough oil so we crank open the windshield of the International for a while, until we get used to the smell. Werner is glad it's a straight shot to the stockyards, no reloading the truck to get around the weight restrictions they enforce in the spring. Sometimes Werner and Lodder have to reload on highway crossroads or on the outskirts of towns, to keep from losing their hauler's licenses.

Werner settles into the corner of the cab like he owns the whole world, legs sticking out, foot on the gas pedal, belly bumping up against the wheel, big thermos right next to the long wobbling shift lever that rises up out of the floor. He holds onto the silver steering wheel knob with his left hand, and with his right, pulls a can of Copenhagen from his bib overall pocket where the can has worn a faded circle. He's driving with his knee, *no hands*, stuffing a load of snuff behind his lower lip that every twenty miles or so he empties with his finger and flings out the window. A few black drops of wet snuff shine in his bushy not-so-red beard by the light of the dashboard gauges. He hands me a stick of Juicy Fruit, a whole one, then reaches back behind the seat with his left hand for his pint, that every fifteen minutes or so he takes a bump from. Each time he raises the bottle in my direction, to ask if I need a drink. I shake my head. When he needs to *shpuk*, he winds up, leans back, and shoots a gob through the steering wheel into the hole where the steering column goes through the floor. Over the years, this hole has gotten bigger and bigger, the metal rusting away from the splattered juice. Through it you can see the road flashing by in the yellow light from the headlights and I know this much: I could ride forever.

Once we're on the tar road, a jack comes flying out of Magnus's busch and he starts all over again about what a good hunter I am. Suddenly I don't want Werner knowing about double stitches and Stricknadeln and the soft murmur of my sisters' voices, not knowing what he would think about that.

I've known the Schmolz brothers all my life. Lodder let me ride around on his back when I was little. I didn't know Werner that well, until the year we were selling grain right from the field. My father hired him to drive our pickup truck back and forth to the elevator, just the kind of job Werner liked—making money while sitting down. We would sit in the truck and I'd play with the crickets I'd find piled up in the corners of the grainbox. Some of them were so mangled from going through the combine that I would put them out of their misery. The doors would be wide open for the wind to pass through as Werner cleaned his long yellow claw fingernails with the point of a jackknife. His big yellow horse teeth would rip into a plug of Red Man that came in an ugly tight rectangle that looked like it'd been glued together with spit. As the wind moved, the sour smell of plug went past my nose and drifted out over the oats stubble into the sky above.

The drone of the engine almost has me nodding off when Werner tells me open the glove box. His big paw snuffles around in a pile of Baby Ruths until it comes up with a Payday, a big one. He offers it to me and I say no because I can see he wants it. He says help yourself, there's a 7-Up bar in there somewhere if you don't like Baby Ruth.

The candy bar wakes me up. I get him started on Leavenworth, where he did ten months, cleaning out of the mulebarns for the U.S. Army. He and Philipp Lendler got nabbed for running moonshine—Minnesota 13—the best in the state. No, he didn't see Capone though Capone was there all the time Philipp and Werner were. Werner just got to see the back ends of mules and was he glad to see the last of those sumbitches, thank you. He wipes his mouth with the back of his hand and slides the bottle back behind the seat.

We're just passing St. Cloud, which is about as far as I'd ever come in the world, and now it's behind us. From a distance, the lights of the Cities brighten the sky. Werner tells me to watch real close now and finally he jabs a Baby Ruth at a clump of trees by the side of the road. That's where a ninety-foot long blue flying saucer, not really a saucer more like a long blue train made of light, followed him one night for twenty-three miles until he was able to shake it approaching Anoka. He had a double deck of pigs in back, squealing for all they're worth; until the blue thing finally backed off and disappeared into the night sky like it was never there. We drive for while not saying much, until we hear bellering in back. We stop to check what's going on but can't see anything wrong. We stand by the edge of the road, side by side, and piss into the ditch, Werner lifting a leg and letting one fly like he's so good at.

As we get closer and closer, the lights fill the sky and the big puffy clouds are almost pinkish white in an almost black sky. There are more cars than I've ever seen. It's almost eleven-thirty when we start going around the city on back roads, Werner knowing exactly where he's going. We pass a big wooden stilty thing along the road that Werner answers is a ski-jump where people tie barrel staves on their feet and fly through the air and land in a heap, not something he thinks he would do, pour me another cup of that coffee, here's a whole stick unless you want the 7-Up bar someone gave me but I don't care for, maybe I'll throw it away, it's so old.

Finally we pull into the stockyards Gregor's never seen, with pens as far as I can see. Steam is rising from them like they're on fire but Werner says it's just animal heat and heat from manure piles. Through the steam, I see the packing house, lit up by a thousand bulbs, where livestock is butchered for city people. Not like us, we do it ourselves, salting and smoking big *schinken* in the smokehouse to give us enough fried pork to last through the hot summer.

There's a whole line of trucks waiting to unload. Werner pulls over to the side and we get out of the hot oily cab into the cold night air that smells like you put your nose into something, and like some kind of tallow or grease. Cattle beller and hogs squeal and the trucks roar away in the night. Right away there's a steer fight, in the back of a small truck on high skinny tires, that rocks the truck until a small man in a long coat to his ankles climbs up the rack and stops it with a cattle prod. We go to a side door and Werner steps into big hellos from everybody. I stand out of the way like my mother told me. The smell is starting to feel like a lump caught in my throat. There's a lot of laughing and backslapping, the two bottles in the brown paper bag clanking, Werner knowing his way around the big city. I can almost feel the stench on my skin. We go back out and pull around the long line of trucks and unload our load of steers ahead of dirty looks and angry cuss words; this isn't tatting. We get the yellow consignment sheet and the lot number that's put on the steers' flanks with blue greasepaint. Werner says he's tired and is going straight to bed for a change.

We go to the hotel that doesn't look at all like the lobby of the St. Germain in St. Cloud, which I have looked at through the glass door. This entrance is a little dirty and the floor has bits of straw pasted to it, with shiny dirt that's been walked over many times. The man knows Werner like a brother and sorry there aren't two beds side by side, the steer market topping out like it is. Every mothertrucker is here for the night, fifty cents a bed. Werner tells me to put my money away; he'd take care of it. We go up the steep steps past a sign that says no lights, quiet please, into a big dark room with maybe eighty beds all lined up. The dim light comes from small red lightbulbs, like in a brooder house but up high on the ceiling. That's the only light in the place, except for dirty yellow light coming in through big windows that look like they've never been washed. Through these windows come the roar of the trucks and bellering of cattle and light from a thousand bulbs on the packing house. The light streams in through the dirt like sunshine through a church window but there's no incense floating here. Just cigarette smoke drifting like fog about three feet above the beds from little knots of men, all truckers, I guess. They're gathered around a beer case here, a quart there, passing it around, shooting dice and playing cards in the squares of light on the floor, murmuring, knirpsing almost, like chickens in the winter night, a low dirty laugh thrown in here and there.

Werner finds two empty beds, his by the wall, mine towards the middle. He tells me again to yell if any cocksuckers start bothering me. I tell him don't worry, thinking I'd played with field crickets all my life so I can take on any cocksuckers that might come crawling beady-eyed up my bedpost. Just to be on the safe side, I fall asleep with my arm out of the bed, holding my shoe, that for sure is heavy enough to squash even the biggest cocksucker. How big could they be?

A couple of times in the night I wake up when somebody drunk bumps the beds and swears like a true trucker. The stockyard smell drifts through the room like cigarette smoke. Still no cocksuckers and my arm is cold, so I put the shoe down where I can get at it. I check my Lone Ranger wallet under the pillow which has sharp chicken feathers that poke your face while you sleep.

It's light when I wake up and the long room is almost empty. There are just a few people schnarchsing under blankets that I notice have US Army stamped on them in black. I wonder if it makes Werner think about Leavenworth. I take my wallet and go over to where his bed is. He's still asleep but wakes up as I stand next to his bed. He looks at me like he's seen a ghost, but finally he remembers he brought me here.

We cross the street to have breakfast, eggs frying on a flat stove, cooks in dirty aprons flipping huge sheets of fried potatoes and breaking eggs, their hands blurring in the steam rising from coffee pots the size of milker buckets. I have the eggs and two orders of toast made with store bought bread and my first cup of coffee without milk, my mother always pouring in the milk at home. Suddenly my brother Gregor, and all the work and tatting seem far away. Werner won't let me pay and now he's already spent seventy-five cents on me. Maybe I'll just leave three quarters in the glove box or buy him some plug. I check my front pocket for my red and blue Lone Ranger wallet—yes it's there.

He takes me up some steps, to what he calls a catwalk, which goes over the pens of cattle that are being held and moved and sorted and looked at by buyers in long yellow coats and high black rubber boots. The catwalk goes to the office where Werner is everybody's friend. The office overlooking the pens is mostly glass windows and white paint, the only close to clean place I've seen since I left home. There's a stack of wood, red oak from the looks of it, and a potbelly stove that is red-hot and dirty and has, of all things, big smoking pieces of meat held onto the hot stovepipe with wire. Juice oozes down the pipe and sizzles the closer it gets to the hot stove, leaving a thick collar of old dried blood just above the firebox. Werner says the drovers like their meat only warm and that sometimes they drink blood, warm blood, *he's seen it.* I know I'm in the big city now.

We get directions to see our steers, over there toward the northwest corner of the yard, where we can only go by catwalk. Werner nudges me, pointing down, there's Gravel Gertie. I look down and see a drover in high boots with the usual eight-foot whip, but this one you can tell from behind is a lady, her big *schinken* filling out what look like my father's Sunday pants. She's driving three or four baloney bulls ahead of her. The bulls, not used to being around other bulls, try to butt at each other but she's got control of them. Her whip flicks out to catch the leader on the shoulder and the bull turns like a calf in a ring, because she's been doing it since the war started and she's the last lady working in the yards.

We walk by a pen full of down stock, then a pen filled with rheumy-looking cattle, noses dripping, others with legs twisted. Werner says, it's from falling in the truck. Load 'em tight, it don't happen. Too bad, he says, people gotta eat.

Our steers sold early and we missed it. The bidding is still hot and heavy. The market is expected to rise for a few more days Werner says. We go off to the place where they write the checks and Werner picks up his share too.

We go back to the truck in the big parking lot and take it over to hose out the manure and straw, our check peeping out of Werner's bib pocket, right next to the faded snuff ring. That done, we head over to a liquor warehouse where we help load cases and cases of gin, vodka, rum and scotch into the truck for Meinulph to sell to the Protestants from the neighboring dry county back home.

We leave the liquor place and right away see an accident of three cars all banged together, with lights flashing on the police cars. They close the road. Werner swears when they make us take a different road back around the city. We end up driving past thousands of houses, some really big, others really small; the whole house not much bigger than our kitchen. Werner swears a long sad string so I think he's lost but I don't say anything because he doesn't either. I'm getting a bit worried now because Werner looks confused. I catch him looking up at the sky like he's looking for the sun or a sign of some kind and he looks at me out of the corner of his eye. I don't let on I see him, because I certainly don't know where we are; besides, I thought he knew. Suddenly I see the stilty thing off in the distance, and tell him. He whoops out a happy string of cusswords this time, so I know he's not worried anymore. He reaches into the glove box and hands me a Payday and tells me what a good boy I am and how glad he is to have me along. We drive past more thousands of cars, the smoke from their exhaust pipes rising in the frozen air like a slough fire. Finally we get to the stilty thing, which looks a little pale in the the weak sun but we're still plenty glad. And I've got a lot to tell my brother Gregor, who will never, ever, ever, catch up to me now.

Out of Hand

We had electricity in our barn just for light and to run the vacuum pump for the milking machines—until the day my father brought home a used radio. It cost fifteen dollars. He built a shelf for it, high enough so the cows walking under it wouldn't bump it. When he hooked the antenna to the long row of iron stanchions, we could get Berlin on it. Their German seemed fast and complicated, with words we didn't recognize because we'd come to America a hundred years ago. Usually, though, we listened to the same thing every night: six o'clock news with Lowell Thomas on WCCO, six-thirty Polka Time on WNAX Yankton, South Dakota, seven o'clock the Lone Ranger on 'CCO; our ears were cocked for the hoof beats over the clicking sound of the milkers.

Below the radio, next to the gutter shovels, my father hung a strap for when my brother and I got out of hand. When we were little, our mother would spank us if we needed it. As we got older, there were times when spanking wasn't enough. He made the strap himself, from a one-inch-square piece of wood about two feet long. Along the length of it, and extending about twenty inches beyond the wood, was an inch-wide strip of leather, actually a section he took from the reins of an old harness that hung in the rafters of the machine shed. Playing in the busch instead of working, or carelessly feeding the calves too much milk and making them sick, could get you a whipping you would remember. It was his job, he did it, and we trusted him not to get carried away with it. Sometimes when he wasn't around, I'd take the strap off the nail and whack the walls of the barn with it. What a sound it made!

About this time we were low on cats, just a white tom which was my father's favorite, and a few others. My father had heard from the parish housekeeper that, in the evening, Father Reiter would sit on his porch in his cassock with a .410 shotgun across his knees, shooting any cat that came near his huge birdhouses. My father had seen some of our cats up by the church, so he was sure that's what happened to them.

In the evening, the white tom was in the habit of sitting on the high flat radio to enjoy the warmth coming from the vacuum tubes. Sometimes the tom would jump down from the radio to my father's shoulder. My father would walk with the cat perched up there, his hand just hesitating near the cat, lest the tom lose his balance. My father walked gracefully, as if he were proud the cat had chosen only him.

One day a neighbor brought over a gunny sack of nineteen identical gray cats, four litters of cats from four gray sister cats, sired by the gray grandfather cat. The neighbor, Josef Lendler, and his boy Ebbie, had caught them in an abandoned barn near old Schuler's place. The cats had never seen a human but that one time when they were being put into a dusty yowling sack. When Ebbie dumped the sack on the barn floor, the screeching cats shot from the neck of the bag in long gray blurs of light.

My brother and I patiently set out pans of milk trying to draw them out of the haymow. They'd never seen milk, so it was hard. Finally we caught one and locked it in the milk house until it was addicted to milk. Eventually the rest began to lurk around, drinking milk and making their livings.

Two months later, because of the new dairy regulations, we had the inside of the barn sprayed to kill off flies. The whitewash had DDT in it. The little gray cats must have thought there was milk on the walls because they licked the whitewash with their pink tongues. The next morning they were all lying stiff, scattered around the barn. A hard lesson. My brother and I started burying them with a shovel but it was too much and we put the rest in the manure spreader. That left us right where we started and there was more grumbling about Father Reiter and his .410.

One night we were doing the evening chores and my father was just ready to check the milkercups on the cow in front of the radio when the high flat box buzzed with static. As my father turned around, the white tom leaped off the radio to land on his shoulder. Instead, he landed on my father's face, all claws at the ready for a firm grip. The tom's back feet dug in right below his eyes and ripped downward across his cheeks and chin and down his neck to his shirt collar. The front feet knocked off his chores cap and raked across his forehead down to his eyebrows. The tom hung on in fear, yowling as my father struck at him with both hands. Finally he grabbed the cat's neck and flung him to the floor. The tom landed on the concrete behind the gutter. My father, his face streaming gobs of blood and flesh, reached blindly for the long-handled gutter shovels that hung next to the strap he used on us. His groping hand fell on the strap instead. He chased the terrified tom as fast as he could, arms whacking at the streaking dodging cat he loved, all the while swearing the most terrible oaths. The panicked cat jumped head first into a corner. My father struck at him blindly but the strap kept hitting the corner wall above the cat's head. Finally the cat escaped through the door, never to be seen again. Wild-eyed, my father turned, breathing hard, blood seeping red into his shirt. "You two want something?" he gasped. We stood up straight, our hands at our sides and shook our heads.

"*Nein, nichts,*" we said, "we don't want nothing."

Rimpel-Zimpel

I wade through the elastic yellow morning air. Tiny insects, dewy grass, floating seeds, specks of pollen, even the bright leaves of early summer bob in my wake as I walk toward the corncrib. The sound of Cletus ringing the Angelus bell drifts across the fields from town. I lean the five-tined fork against the slatted walls and spread ground corn from two coffee cans on the spot where I'll turn the ground. Earthworms come to corn. The soft dirt cools my bare feet and the digging is easy. After ten minutes, I put two cans of worms in the trunk of the car next to the rods and reels and bamboo poles.

I know I should be working, filling the feeders in the brooder house, but I wonder what Maggie is doing. I turn toward the house, toward Maggie, and the smell of frying bacon that hangs in the air.

My mother stands at the black cookstove making breakfast. Next to her frying pans, three heavy flatirons are warming on the stove top. During the summer, the ironing is done while meals are being cooked, so the house doesn't heat up more than necessary. My sisters are sweeping and cleaning and taking care of the babies. Maggie, our hired girl, is already ironing. I pull a chair next to her and watch her heft the weight of the flat irons. At first she hurries the hot iron lightly across a dress, then slows and presses harder as the iron cools. She sighs and looks over at me. Her red lips glisten in the morning light as she moves. She turned seventeen in May, nine years ahead of me.

"Why're you wearing lipstick, Maggie? It's not Friday."

She looks up at the calendar, counting the days until Friday's dance. The Bishop doesn't allow dances on Saturday night, a way to get people to Sunday Mass.

"Ebbie, don't you have something better to do?" she asks. "It's twenty minutes until breakfast. Why don't you put some straw in those nests? The eggs are bouncing on bare wood. I'm tired of all the cracked eggs."

She never complained like this before Reiner came. She looks down and sees my toes lifting a loose corner of the kitchen linoleum. Last year we covered the oak floor with black and white squares of linoleum. The dampness rising from the rainwater cistern under the kitchen floor loosens the glue and the linoleum expands. To glue it back down, the edges of the squares have to be trimmed with a razor blade to make them fit, an ugly job my mother usually does. She looks at my mother and her lips look like she's going to say Juletta, but she doesn't say anything.

"But why the lipstick, Maggie?" I like the sound of her name and repeat it. "It's for Reiner, isn't it, Maggie? You're wearing it for Reiner, aren't you, Maggie. Maggie?"

"What's it to you? Just let me finish my ironing."

She stares at a corner of the ceiling, brushing her dark hair out of her eyes. She's been grouchy ever since Reiner came to work for us. Yesterday she threw a bucket of water at him while he was washing the milk cans. We used to talk all the time. I want to ask her about the movies again but I know I had better wait.

I sneak upstairs for a few minutes to the "rimpel-zimpel." That's how the little ones say Gerümpel Zimmer, the junk room. I tiptoe past the long bedroom Maggie shares with Sarah and Bea and my other three sisters. I hear Flo talking in there. The door to Reiner's tiny room is open, the bed still unmade. I lift my feet over the squeaky board in front of the junk-room door. I sit on the floor of the "rimpel-zimpel," my back against a creaking wicker basket full of flannel sheets. My hand goes under the rusted tin washtub for the book I keep hidden there. The book must have come with the house. During summer vacation, the only books we have are prayer books. This book has no front cover, the back cover is green. I skip past Apollo, Vulcan, and Arthur's Table and turn to the story about Siegfried fighting the dragon. When I try to imagine Siegfried, I think of the plaster St. Michael mounted above the doors of the church. I turn the brittle yellow pages carefully and am surprised again at how complicated life was then. Our lives are so . . . simple, boring even. I save my favorite story for last, the Song of Roland. I stare at the picture of Roland's long thin figure lying head down in a pass in the mountains, the horn still in his hand, black blood running from an arrow in his chest. Brave to the end. If I had to, I think I could do that. It feels like only a minute until Maggie calls me to breakfast. I take the stairs two at a time.

After breakfast my father, Reiner and I head west on the concrete pavement that connects Highway 4 to Sauk Centre. My father twists the rear-view mirror upward as the morning sun glares off the mirror into his eyes. A quivering rectangle of light vibrates on the gray felt ceiling of the car. Sitting next to my father, Reiner laughs and talks. He's wearing a white T-shirt, his short sleeves rolled up over large muscles. He wears his hair short, though he didn't go to Korea like Romuald. I watch the muscles knot in his neck as he turns to look out of the window.

Under the wheels, the joints between the concrete sections of the highway have spread with the spring thaw. The faster we go the less time between clicks. It hypnotizes me and I nod off. I wake up when my father turns onto the gravel road toward Beecher's on Lily Lake. Beecher has four flat-bottomed boats and an old barn to protect them from winter. Inside the barn are a minnow tank and a Coca-Cola machine with the top cover broken.

A retired farmer, Beecher hobbles around the corner of the barn at the sound of our car. Once I went back there to see what he might be doing. A kitchen chair was tilted up against the barn, facing east into the morning sun. On a rough table lay a knife and eight or ten wooden bears, some completely finished with tiny grooves for fur, others still blocks of wood, square corners, notches forming the legs. I touch them. They're warm from the sun.

There is a winding path, like a cow path, to the lake. I dodge the small puddles from last night's rain. I'm carrying my bamboo pole and the worms. At the end of the path the lake lies almost flat, like a mirror gone soft from the heat, reflecting sheets of light up through the branches of the dark trees.

The dock is a rickety, swaying patchwork of old lumber, some of it rough cut, some with red barn paint showing in the raised grain. To avoid the splinters, I've learned to lift my feet high as I walk, like a rooster parading the hen yard. I choose the boat with the pulley for the anchor rope and claim it with the worm cans. I'm going to catch a huge fish for Maggie.

Reiner carries the minnow bucket into the barn. My father has started to buy minnows for trolling since we've been fishing with Reiner. The second time, my father figured it out: minnows are too cheap to count. He pays for a dozen and Beecher gives him about fifty. Reiner carries the oars on his shoulder like a gun. I yell, "Forward, march." Reiner pulls in his chin and goose steps toward the dock.

My father's nervous yell: Don't run. Like most people he fears water. Once my cousin Bobby stepped off the dock, missed the boat and sank to the bottom. My father threw himself down on the boards, and stuck his arm in the water up to his shoulder, reaching for him. He pulled Bobby out by his overall straps. Going fishing is an act of courage for my father. He sits in the absolute center of the boat. He moves slowly and carefully on the deadly water. He scans the blue sky for a storm cloud. No one here knows swimming.

Today we're making a second try at passing through the channel that leads to a hidden lake, inaccessible because the land around it is owned by just three farmers. There is an old channel, but it's dry most years. With two summers of heavy rain behind us, the lake has risen enough so a boat could almost clear the trees the farmers around the lake have dynamited into the channel to keep outsiders away. There are rumors about the size of the sunfish, the huge gape-mouthed crappies, fat northerns and a fish as long as a boat that cruises the lake just below the surface. I've even heard that there are bears.

The oarlocks creak as Reiner leans into the oars, his big boots braced against the ribs at the bottom of the boat. As he leans forward, the back of his t-shirt tightens almost to bursting. A whirlpool eddies up from the clear water; his shirt goes slack and his shoulder blades reappear. His thick wrists never tire, his oars never raise a splash, even when we race a storm cloud back to the dock. When we go fishing, he's not our hired man anymore. My father does not speak of work but jokes easily with him.

The water is black under the lily pads. We glide through them searching the shallow bottom for the slight channel we'd seen before. We can't find it but Reiner is set on it. We wouldn't even be looking, if it weren't for Reiner.

We ease forward until the bottom of the boat is resting on the ooze. Frogs stare at us from the lily pads. A dragonfly lands on the tip of a furled fishing rod, good luck going to waste. Reiner turns to look ahead and sees a shallow furrow leading to an opening in the fallen trees. He tests the bottom with an oar. The muck is a foot deep. He unlaces his boots and pulls off his socks.

"What do you think you're doing, Reiner?" my father asks.

Reiner's long white feet look dead in the sunlight. He wiggles his toes and puts one foot over the side.

"Reiner, what are you doing?"

"Don't worry, Josef, I'll just help it along."

My father and I both yell, "You'll tip the boat."

The water lilies bob, their creamy blossoms winking in the sunlight. Water nearly ships over the top of the boat and suddenly Reiner is standing next to us like a giant. He slogs around to the back and tells me to move there so the nose of the boat will come up. He grabs the handholds on the back of the boat, lifting and pushing us toward the opening.

We approach the dynamited trees. Mosquitoes rise up in towering swarms. Someone has been here years before us. There are old saw marks on the fallen trees where branches have been cut away. We duck our heads as limbs glide over us. Tree trunks, half-drowned, flank the boat. We lie almost flat. Reiner is bent double, grunting us over submerged trunks. There are no bent weeds here: we're the first to enter from this side. We pass the last big tree and the view opens up and before us lies a new lake, surrounded by low hills covered with dark oak trees. No one we know has seen it before. Secretly, I name it Lake Maggie.

We don't know where to fish but decide on a likely spot not far from a bed of cattails. My father and Reiner bet on the first fish—the loser buys the winner a drink at the saloon on the way home. My hook is baited and my line is in the water before we stop. As my father spits his Copenhagen into the water for good luck, my four-foot bamboo bends nearly double under the weight of a sunny the size of my father's huge hand.

We fish for two hours, alternately whooping and shouting in amazement at the size of the fish that are years larger than the fish in Lily Lake, then shushing each other as if expecting the farmers to catch us on their lake. Even the scrappy yellow bellies look brawny, like another fish altogether.

In two hours we're way over the limit, our pails filled to the top. We're worried about the game warden we'd seen from Beecher's dock. We debate putting some of the sunfish on stringers and hiding them in a jacket. As we're leaving, my father doesn't panic when Reiner steps over the side. We creep back through the channel. Reiner claims the boat is heavier and harder to lift. I remind them that I caught the first fish.

On the way home we stop at the saloon in Spring Hill. My father's Uncle Martin is on a spree, drinking like a two-fisted man, according to Reiner, even though he's got only the one hand. I'm eight but my father buys me my first glass of beer over the bar, ten cents. We say nothing to Meinulph about the new lake; instead, we complain about the fishing in Lily Lake and talk of driving south to Hawick to try Long Lake there. I spin around on the high barstool and look out across the street at the dancehall where Maggie goes on Friday nights.

Meinulph runs his hand across his bald head and asks Reiner who he took home from the last Friday's dance. Reiner shakes his head, laughs, then orders another round.

As we turn into the yard, I see Reiner glance over at the house. Maggie's face disappears behind the white curtain. My father pulls the car into the shade of the busch that surrounds the farmyard. We unload the pails of fish under the huge poplar tree where an old table and chairs stand. My father sharpens his fish-cleaning knife on the *schleif-stein.* As I crank the heavy round stone, the yellow-red sparks from his knife die in the green grass. Reiner and I scale the fish, trying to stay ahead of my father, who lops off heads and guts fish faster than the two of us can scale them. A soft breeze blows the sweet smell of alfalfa through the shady woods. When we finish, my father lets me pick off the fish scales dried to his arms.

Maggie opens the door a crank then quickly steps back in. In a minute, she comes out again and calls Reiner over to the lilac bushes. They talk. I'm listening through the sound of the fluttering poplar leaves overhead, but can't hear what they're saying. Reiner laughs; she slaps his face. I want to run over there. Reiner laughs again and makes a face like Buster Keaton. He ambles back, grinning, saying he expects he'll be going to the dance alone on Friday. He goes into the shed for the paint brushes and paint. I want to ask Maggie when we can see the movies again but this is not the time.

Last Christmas, Maggie invited our whole family to her parents' house to watch movies. Maggie and five of her brothers and sisters all work as hired men and girls. The rest of the kids are still at home. Together, the older kids bought a movie projector, a white screen and reels of movies to go with it: Buster Keaton, Laurel and Hardy, and the Three Stooges. We laughed like we were from Fergus, watching Buster Keaton in a Model T being chased by a train down the railroad track, then driving through a barn, collapsing it, chickens flying everywhere. We watched the movie backwards when it was being rewound. It was even funnier. Keaton 'falling' upwards left us gasping for breath.

Reiner comes out of the shed swinging a half-empty five-gallon bucket of paint. The cover is off and he windmills it at the end of his arm five or six times. A faint outline of Maggie's hand glows on his cheek. I am hoping the paint will land on his head but it doesn't.

Two weeks later, Maggie is still angry at him. It's Friday night and Reiner leaves for the dance alone in his cream-colored '41 Ford. Maggie waits for her oldest brother Romuald to pick her up. Before Reiner came around, I remember watching Maggie put on her lipstick and once, impulsively, she bent down and kissed me, leaving a scarlet trace on my cheek from her soft lips. Now Maggie storms out of the house without a word, a trail of perfume snapped short by the slamming of the screen door. I follow the scent, part of me happy, part sad.

In the midsummer gap between haying and the cutting of barley, we resume the secret plundering of the hidden lake. There is no end to the fierce fish hiding there. We begin to think of ourselves as fishermen, though we know it is the bounty of the lake that accounts for our success. My father talks about buying a three-horse motor so that we could fish longer. Reiner says nothing. I think he enjoys the reach and pull of rowing. His white t-shirt shows faded specks of red paint high on his shoulders.

Reiner and Maggie have stopped fighting. One evening I spot them walking the lane near the pasture, their heads together. The heat of the summer drains the color from the sky and the fire from their arguments. In July, the barley turns a reddish gold and every passing breeze reveals its shape on the rolling fields. My father is preparing the grain binder, sealing the slatted canvas with varnish to keep mildew from rotting the fabric. Reiner has finished the overhang of the haymow, his extension ladder roped to the carrier track forty-two feet above the ground. Only the high metal cupolas remain unpainted.

As I trudge out to the potato field behind the busch, Reiner is setting up a tall stepladder on the sloping peak of the barn next to the high cupola that vents the moisture from the hay mow. I want to stay and watch him put on the silvery aluminum paint. My mother, a firm grip on my ear, insists it's time to go after the potato bugs attacking the potato plants. My sister Bea and I trudge out to the dusty potato field carrying empty horse liniment bottles.

The long rows seem to stretch to the horizon. We hunch over in the dust, checking the undersides of the prickly leaves for the black-and-yellow striped bugs. Bea thinks it's fun catching them. I say nothing, holding my bottle upright so I can't feel their knobby heads bumping against my thumb. I mutter when I notice the potatoes are beginning to push up out of the ground, the skin turning green from the sun. That means at least two days of haufing the dirt up around the plants to protect the potatoes from sunburn. I keep an occasional eye on a chicken hawk circling above the brooder house where the white pullets dot the yard like so many Sunday dinners. Bea yells at me to get busy. She can't wait to get back and fill the bottles with kerosene and set fire to the bugs. I wonder why we can't cork the bottles and let them starve to death.

As we turn the corner of the busch, I hear Reiner laughing and Maggie shouting. She's standing in the center of the yard, her hand shielding her eyes. We look up to see he's finished the first cupola. The new aluminum paint makes it look even larger. Reiner is standing high on the ladder pointing up at the letters R-L-M in foot-high red letters across the broad band near the top of the cupola.

He shouts down to her, "I already told you, Maggie. It's "Reiner Loves Maggie."

Maggie is trying to sound angry. "Paint over it, Reiner, please. Please?" She is laughing, almost doubled over.

"No, I'm leaving it. And it's too high for anyone else to reach. It'll be up here forever, for everybody to see."

I've never seen Maggie's face so lit up. She shakes her long hair and looks over at us, blushing. She runs over and hugs us, laughing as she does, kissing us both. She looks back up at Reiner, waves at him then runs to the steps of the house and turns to see how it looks from there.

The barley has been cut and is drying in long rows of shocks that weave drunkenly up and down the rolling stubble fields. Uncle Willem pushes my father to cut the oats so he won't have to bring his threshing machine and crew to our farm twice. There's hardly time for fishing anymore, but we decide we could go once more if we went early enough. We get up at four and drive through the half-light the fifteen miles to the lake. Beecher's house is dark but he knows us. We take a boat from the dock and Reiner rows us toward the channel. In the western sky, heavy clouds are moving in. The first rays of the sun barely clear the heavy stand of trees on the eastern shore. Above our heads, white gulls wheel in great circles. They turn black as they dip into the darkness, then brighten to intense gold as they rise up into the almost horizontal rays of the vibrating sunlight overhead.

The first drops of rain hit as Reiner steps into the muck. My father says we should turn back. Reiner insists we go on, that the storm will pass to the south. We anchor at our now-favorite spot. The fish are biting ferociously. Within minutes we have ten fish. They bite before the line straightens in the water. A cold blast of wind proves Reiner wrong. Big drops bounce off the flat bottom of the boat. The clouds roll low above the trees and the sun vanishes behind the heavy cover of gray-black clouds. Reiner's rod doubles over. He whoops as a huge northern fights at the end of his line. He stands. My father's eyes grow large. He barks at Reiner to sit down. Reiner sees the look on my father's face and sits. My father pulls out a crappie half as long as his arm. I catch an old sunfish thick as a plank. We put the worm cans under the seats to keep the rain from filling them. Water sloshes at our feet.

The rain is cold, but pulling up fish is keeping us warm. A bolt of lightning splits the sky. My father opens his mouth to say something about getting off the lake, just as the tip of his fishing rod dives down into the water. A crack of thunder follows that nearly drowns his surprised yell, lifting all of us from our seats. He's fighting a big fish. Reiner curses as fish flop around his ankles in the boat. The sharp fin of a yellow-belly jabs my hand and blood oozes out but is immediately diluted by the rain. The rolling thunder covers our whooping and hollering. My father combines the two cans of worms and bails water with the empty can. At the same time, he's landing a fighting crappie.

The pails are so full that fish flop out as fast as we throw them in. We've been fishing forty-five minutes in the pouring rain but it feels like five minutes. We have a hundred and fifty fish already. Over the crack of a nearby lightning strike, Reiner yells to keep fishing: they don't pay game wardens enough to come out in weather like this. The wind shifts and the rain comes in at a slant as the center of the storm comes back for another pass. Lightning shivers the sky and the boom of thunder moves toward us. My father can't stand it any longer. He orders me to pull the anchor. Reiner objects but then leans into his work when a bolt of lightning raises the hair on our heads. The smell of dynamite is in the air. We plow through the lily pads and weeds toward the nearest shore and pull up to a steep embankment. Through the driving rain, we scramble up to a heavy growth of trees. Reiner carries the anchor up the slope to keep the waves from taking out the boat.

We huddle together, struck dumb by the ferocity of the storm. The air is so full of rain, I'm surprised we can still breathe. White caps break on the shore in the semi-darkness. I think of the safe old rimpel-zimpel and Roland's long thin figure. Under my breath, I mumble the Act of Contrition, in case I'm killed by lightning. O Most Sacred Heart of Jesus. Most Sacred Heart of Jesus, Most Sacred Heart of Jesus. I repeat the words, hoping God won't send me to hell with His holy name on my lips. Now is the time to be brave to the end. Suddenly I want to go home. I would give the fish back to the lake if that's what it took for the storm to pass.

The pace of the rain lessens and the wind quiets. When the rain stops, we stumble and slide down the long wet grass of the embankment. Fish are still flopping around in the water at the bottom of the boat. We cast a glance upward before getting back in. The fish and our gear have to be taken out to tip the water out of the boat. Nobody speaks until we clear the channel. Reiner's steady rowing gets us back to the safety of Beecher's dock.

It's Saturday afternoon. Maggie is on her knees in the kitchen, trimming the linoleum; the smell of glue hangs in the air. It's a terrible job, but Maggie hums to herself as I come in. She smiles. I haul the old heavy flatirons out of a cabinet for her. I can't count how often I've stubbed my toes on the flatirons in the night on my way to the bathroom. When she finishes trimming the edges and puts down the glue, Maggie puts all her weight on each flatiron to press down the freshly-glued squares.

That night, a cry from one of my sisters wakes me. I hear Flo hopping around the kitchen, holding her toe. I can't help but smile when she stubs it again. She sniffles her way upstairs and the house falls silent. A gust of wind shakes the tree outside my window. The moon setting through the moving branches creates a movie over my head. I can remember almost all of the Buster Keaton movie and I run it backwards through my head. There is a creak and I think the wind has picked up, but the sound is coming from the hall. Footsteps on the bare wood floor. A board creaks in front of the rimpel-zimpel, a familiar sound. I hear Reiner's door open and shut. I listen to the dull murmur of two voices but I can't keep my eyes open and I drift away.

First Impressions

The first time she saw him, Anna fell in love with the principal's son. From afar, of course, though once he did smile down at her as they bumped each other in a crowded hall. He had come to her school from the Cities when his father became the principal. Carlo was so tall, and dark, a wonderfully foreign-looking Italian. Northern, he always added, she wasn't sure why. He stood out among all the Germans: six-foot-two, long hair lightly oiled and those serious glasses that made him look older than he was. While the other girls giggled over Elvis, Anna said nothing.

Anna could see by the way Carlo held himself that he was going places, places she'd never see. He walked in the hallways with teachers, his father's employees, bending down to listen to their answers, nodding his head slowly, as if weighing the truth of what he heard. Sometimes he wore a suit and tie—to school. So tall and thin. He was only a junior, a year ahead of her, and already he wanted to be a *college* principal.

Carlo.

Every afternoon she watched him from the bus. He would come out of the school, surrounded by his friends, the girls looking up into his gray-green eyes, the boys lightly tapping the shoulder of his letter jacket. A little gold football, and a basketball shone on the high school letter on his chest.

But today, instead of turning left to go to the principal's fine house next to the school, Carlo and Bill, Anna's cousin, walked toward the bus where Anna sat. Anna's sister Barbara said Carlo was going to write an article and take pictures for the school yearbook about Bill's ag project, which was weighing and recording milk production for the Dairy Herd Improvement Association. This was the first of three visits. Carlo was carrying a leather valise. He was staying overnight and, Barbara added: he'll, be, on, our, bus.

Bill, Anna and Barbara lived at the end of the bus line, fifty-five minutes from the school, morning and afternoon. The high yellow bus pulled away from the school with a roar, then wound through the rolling farmland, sunlight glancing off the banks of snow left from a mild winter.

Everyone was on their best behavior, as if Carlo were judging their lives. After Anna's friend got off, she turned sideways in her seat, resting her head on the cold glass of the window behind her. Out of the corner of her eye, she could see how straight he sat, how seriously he spoke, and how easily he smiled.

She watched him turn from side to side, examining the fields and farmyards. He would turn to look at something outside and she looked to see what it was and it was worth looking at: the Klempers' new grain bins, her Aunt Bernadette sorting through the leftovers of her woodpile. He looked at the tall, still leafless windbreaks that blocked the everlasting snow into long drifts, and at the perfect farmyard of the fanatic Schulers, where, in their woods, under the snow, no twig lay. The things he looked at took on a special glow, as if they counted for something.

As the bus emptied, the rest of the kids moved to empty seats close to Carlo. Anna hung back, knowing that for the last part of the ride it would just be the four of them, Bill, Barbara, Anna and Carlo.

They were coming to the hard part now: they needed to keep Carlo from seeing the mess at the Schefters' place on the left side of the road. They clattered over the frost heaves near the creek, bouncing nearly to the ceiling of the bus.

"Slow down, Hilarius," Bill yelled, "you'll put us through the roof."

Hilarius had driven an ambulance in the war. Anna could see his ragged cloth on the driver's seat that covered the wheelbarrow inner tube he sat on for his hemorrhoids. Please, she thought, no sermons on how sitting on cold rocks causes hemorrhoids.

Carlo was laughing now. His eight even knuckles showed on the seat ahead of him. She could see Bill tensing up a bit and start to talk about the new Harvestore silos on the horizon out of the right window. Even the other kids knew they had to distract him. They pointed at the blue silos too, explaining the airtight glass lining, the fresh color of the silage even after a long winter, their words tumbling out of their mouths, piling up at his feet.

Carlo's eyes followed the pointing fingers. Anna turned her head slightly to see what he was missing. The Schefters' yard looked like a mudslide of broken rusting machinery and gray buildings. The porch screen door lay askew on the steps, held by one twisted hinge. Three large dogs had backed a flapping sow into a grain box and were barking furiously. The windmill, thick with old vines, had fallen across the tilted shambles of the smokehouse and caved in the roof. She caught a glimpse of what looked like a bunch of skinny pigs running loose. Two of the Schefter brats were chasing each other, flinging handsful of mud scooped up from along the mudboards that led from the house to the barn. She glanced back. He was still looking at the silos. He hadn't seen a thing.

Carlo.

Finally it was the four of them, for the last five miles. Casually, Anna walked back to sit with her sister. Bill looked up at her. "Carlo, you know Anna, don't you?"

"We've never formally met, have we, Anna?" he said.

He half-rose and held out his hand. For a second, she had to think which hand she should shake with. She hoped he hadn't noticed. His hand felt soft but muscular.

"I've heard teachers talking about your ability," he said, He smiled easily. She blushed slightly and vowed she'd study even harder. She sat in the seat across from him.

He looked around the empty bus. "It's sort of nice, now that it's quiet, isn't it?" He looked at Barbara who gulped then agreed with him.

"It's a long ride for you, isn't it?" he asked.

They shook their heads, no, it was fine, being at the end of the line. They were coming down the hill towards their farm and Uncle Jerome's who lived a quarter mile further on. The farm looked fine. She hoped her father had parked the manure spreader behind the busch after he'd worked on the broken beaters. He had.

"So this is your farm, Anna?"

She nodded, thinking that the bus was warmer than usual.

"Everything's so tidy!" Carlo exclaimed. "Well, see you first thing in the morning, Anna. We've got work to do, don't we, Bill?"

Barbara ran ahead to tell her mother about Carlo. Anna just stood at the end of the short driveway, clutching her books. She watched the bus until it got to her Uncle Jerome's farm, where Bill and Carlo got off. Shifting the books to one arm, she picked up a corn cob from the driveway and threw it into the busch. It did look tidy. She just wanted to hug somebody, anybody. He'd called her by name: three times. Sometimes it was so easy. Just that morning her mother had told her: yes, tomorrow you can wear your good dress to school, before you outgrow it altogether. It was all falling into place.

Even her father noticed how happy she was, and for a change supper was quiet and there weren't any arguments. When she finished the dishes they played five hundred until she remembered she wanted to do some extra-credit homework. It was hard to get to sleep. She thought of Carlo, just a quarter mile away.

The next morning she did her chores around the house, kept the babies out of her mother's hair until breakfast was on the table, put Gregor's .22 back into the cabinet, then brushed her own hair until it shone. She changed into her good dress. Her father and brother Gregor came in from milking.

"Going to church, Anna?" Gregor said at the breakfast table.

"No, moron, school. Mom said I can wear this for school now."

He leaned over to her.

"I hear you're pretty excited about this Carlo guy on the bus. So he's writing an article for the newspaper, is he?"

"A feature for the yearbook, moron, not the newspaper. He's interested in everything."

"So I've heard. Sounds like goody-two-shoes to me."

"That's what you know about it. He's going to college, you know." Gregor made a face. She was watching the clock, three more minutes. He's getting on right now.

"C'mon, Barbara, the bus'll be here any minute." She ran to check her hair in the bathroom mirror.

"C'mon, we don't want to be late." She pushed her sister ahead of her to the door. Barbara stopped. Anna pushed again.

"Stop pushing, Annie. There're some pigs out here on the steps. And they're not ours. They look wild."

Anna looked over Barbara's shoulder. Two big skinny pigs stood on the steps, their teeth growing past their jaws like tusks, their backbones like knobs pushing up the skin on their backs. She'd never seen anything like it. More of them crowded on the cement in front of the house. Her sister screamed.

"Willem," Anna heard her mother say, "see what's wrong."

Her father pushed past her. He shoved against the door, knocking one of the pigs off the step. He reached outside and grabbed a garden hoe and brought it down across the second pig's back. The handle splintered and broke. The pig hardly noticed. Her father pushed it off the steps, too. A skinny spotted hog got behind him and suddenly her father was surrounded. He yelled for Gregor. Anna stood slack-jawed. The pigs were so thin, like they hadn't been fed all winter. She'd heard of wild dogs traveling in packs. But pigs? Carlo. She remembered: the bus. Carlo.

The bus pulled up at the end of the short driveway. Barbara pulled Anna out the back door and toward the bus. She stopped. Through the glare of the bus window she could see them, staring, their mouths open. Over the shouting and the squealing pigs, she heard the window of the bus ratchet down. Bill and Carlo looked out. Bill raised his fist and cheered. Carlo sat wide-eyed. Her face burned.

Gregor came running around the back of the house. Willem was swinging wildly with the broken handle. There were at least fifteen. Gregor's head swiveled, looking for a stick, a weapon, anything. He reached down, pulled a loose board from the cellar door and waded into the herd of pigs that had Willem surrounded. Mips and the other dogs came running and joined in. Bill and Carlo laughed and pointed.

Anna stopped and turned on the bus steps. She couldn't believe this was happening right before his eyes. Gregor skidded and fell face forward into the ditch along the driveway. He stood up, spitting dirt. Willem and Gregor were back to back, skinny hump-backed hogs milling around them, their long teeth slicing the air.

"Come on, Anna, let's go." Hilarius spoke behind her.

"Go?" Anna's voice rose. "What are you talking about? My dad needs help."

She handed him the aluminum snow shovel behind the driver's seat and pulled on his arm. Her father yelled for Gregor to get the rifle. Hilarius worked his way toward her father, whacking at the snouts of the crazed hogs, the silver metal of the shovel catching the sunlight. Anna couldn't imagine where the pigs had come from. From up north, or from some isolated farm? Why today? Then she recalled the running pigs at the Schefter's. Those damn Shefters.

Gregor came out of the house with his .22 rifle. Willem and Hilarius were surrounded. Hilarius's ripped pants leg billowed around his ankle, his long underwear turning red from a gash. Anna could see Gregor hesitate, the barrel of the rifle looking for an open target. He fired and a muddy red Duroc at the edge of the pack squealed and turned to look at its backside.

Her father yelled to Gregor.

"Not bird-shot, get the regular shells."

Gregor turned toward the house and tried to kick his way back out of the tangle of pigs at his feet. He fell over a dirty Chester White and lost his footing. The pig ran away with him draped over its back. Anna heard laughing behind her. "Help him, don't just sit there, Carlo," she said. Bill jumped up and ran to the front of the bus. He grabbed a tire wrench from behind the driver's seat. Carlo looked behind the seat too but found nothing at all. He ran back for his suitcase and clattered down the steps after Bill. The battle had moved toward the chicken coop. The noise was terrific, pigs squealing and grunting, Hilarius swearing, the squealing pigs, yelping dogs whirling and grabbing, pigs stumbling over each other.

Bill lumbered into the piled confusion, swinging the cross-shaped tire wrench, jabbing his own leg with every swing. Carlo hovered on the edge, his shoulders hunched up around his ears, holding his ridiculous suitcase. Anna stared at him. A lot of good he was going to do just standing there.

A wide-snouted Poland China headed for Carlo, its lean black-and-white spotted sides rippling as it ran. Carlo swung the leather suitcase around just as the pig reached him. The leather bag connected with a loud thud that scared the pig as much as it hurt him. It ran from the pack toward the road. Barbara cheered and Carlo looked over with a grin as he moved in, cutting a swath with his slashing valise. Her father looked over at Carlo in amazement: the suit, the tie, the suitcase.

Anna ran to the chicken coop and found a long-handled shovel next to the door. Barbara went into the coop, emerging with a wire egg basket half-full of eggs. Anna moved into the fray where she landed two quick blows on a runty Poland China. Barbara fired off one egg after another, catching Hilarius twice. "For Christ's sake, Barbara, stop it," Hilarius laughed, as she swung the empty wire egg basket at a pig just out of her reach.

"Drive 'em toward the road," Willem yelled, "Get 'em the hell out of here." He was rammed from behind and fell forward into the muddy yard as a rush of squealing animals passed over him. Anna couldn't see her father now, just the panicked look on Gregor's face. He was unable to fire a shot. He grabbed the rifle by the barrel and swung the butt into the pack of bodies around him. Carlo kicked and swung his suitcase until he reached her father and pulled him up out of the mud with a jerk.

Ka-Boom! A roar echoed off the buildings. Ka-Boom! On the steps, Anna's mother broke open the smoking 12-gauge shotgun and tossed the empty cartridges aside. She reloaded and fired into the air again. The press of pigs broke open and moved toward the bus. Bill and Carlo were laughing now, swinging at the backsides of the pigs as they chased them out of the yard. The dogs were on their tails, Mips loping along behind, grabbing pigs' tails as he ran.

Anna looked at the ankle-deep mud, at her father's muddy overalls; at Hilarius, breathing hard, with his ripped pants and twisted shovel, egg dripping from his shoulder; at Gregor, his rifle barrel-down on his shoulder, his face smeared with mud; at her mother on the steps, nervous now but grinning with two of Anna's sisters hanging onto her legs, the shotgun crooked over her arm; at Bill with his tire iron and muddied knees, whooping and laughing, his arm around Carlo's shoulders; at Carlo laughing with disbelief, exhilarated, swinging his valise back and forth, his shoes muddied but his suit somehow spotless. Her father looked up from his hand, bleeding from the splintered board.

"Garsh now, what the hell was that about?" he asked. He turned to Carlo. "Who are you? And what are you doing here?"

Carlo smiled, shook his head and held out his hand.

"My name's Carlo. I'm here writing an article about Bill's ag project." He laughed. "To think I almost missed this part of it. I had no idea farming could be so exciting."

Her father's short laugh echoed in the circle. "I've been farming forty years and this is the first time this has happened—must've escaped and gone wild." He shook his head. "A suitcase, huh? That's a good one."

He called to Anna's mother, "Judith, there any coffee left in the pot? We deserve something after all this."

"Oh, no, we don't," Hilarius said. He looked at Bill. "I'll run you back for some clean pants, Bill. Carlo, you clean your shoes and you girls pretty up yourselves. I've got a schedule to meet." He wiped at the egg on his shoulder and looked at Barbara, "You need to work on your aim, young lady."

"But what about your leg, Hilarius?" Carlo asked.

He held up his leg. "This ain't nothing. I was in the war, you know. Nothing the first-aid kit won't fix."

Carlo looked at Anna. "I want to meet your mother, but then we'd better get cleaned up. Hilarius will be back in a few minutes." He smiled and touched her elbow as they walked toward the house. He looked down at her as he spoke.

"So tell me, Anna, is it like this every morning?"

Carlo.

You See What's In Front of You

Surrounded by rolling fields and tidy farmsteads, the church steeple soars above the village to a height of one hundred eighty-three feet. The massive church was built with local field stone, brick, and donated labor in 1900. Statuary, two side altars and the ornately-carved high altar of oak, basswood, and brass were brought from Europe at great expense. The pulpit, with its curving staircase, bears the carved images of the Evangelists: Matthew, Mark, Luke and John, below an intricately carved roof. In the nave of the church, row upon row of long oak pews reflect the optimism and prolific fertility of the Catholic families of eight, ten, or twelve children–the last child accurately marking the onset of menopause of each family's mother.

It was in early June that the midafternoon shadow of the cross fell on the upstairs bedroom windows of the widow Hofer's house where her son Cletus had been napping.

Danny saw Cletus open the front door, step out, and turn, glancing upwards at the shadow of the cross above his head. He turned back to the door and carefully closed it.

Cletus looked at his new shoes, then over to the two boys sitting on a bench in front of the repair shop across the street. With both hands, Cletus pulled down on his grease-monkey cap, the kind with no bill, so the top of his head was squeezed into a round shape that reminded Danny of an eraser on a pencil. Cletus called to his dog, Dewey, who came grinning around the corner. Cletus glanced down at his new shoes again.

Danny and Toby were sitting on the clean bench next to the big door of Irvin's Garage. Toby's broken-nailed left hand played with a coil of wire, his nicotine-browned right held a cigarette. Danny, three years younger, fresh from a haircut, rubbed the short stubble on back of his twelve-year old neck. Squinting through the smoke from the cigarette that angled from his mouth, Toby quickly knelt by the bench. He tied one end of the wire to one leg, then stretched it across the doorway to another bench that held the black imprint of Cletus's backside.

A few weeks earlier, Cletus was squatting to pull a floor jack out from under Jerome's new '56 Ford when Toby slid the flat oil pan behind him, and gave his overalls a gentle tug. Streaming oil from his baggy overalls, Cletus had stomped out of the garage and sulked on the bench.

Cletus called Dewey again. Toby stood quickly and yelled, "Hey, Cletus, ready to race yet?"

Cletus woke up and the goofy grin that creased the black stubble on his moony face disappeared. He patted Dewey's head.

"N-no," he stuttered, "Irvin wants me to c-clear the weeds behind the grotch this afternoon. He said he'd work on my car for me."

Toby yelled across the road. "You're chicken, Cletus. You've always got some excuse."

Cletus didn't seem to hear. He picked up a hand sickle from the step. His new work shoes shone with a fresh coat of harness oil. Dirty fingerprints ringed the outside of an "I like Ike" button that smiled from his shirt. He stopped at the edge of the dusty tar road. His brow furrowed as he looked to the south, past his own house and up the street toward the church and the ball diamond at the end of village. Satisfied, he looked to the north, as if to name each building in view—Meinulph's Saloon, Kellner's Grocery, Kellner's Saloon, the dancehall, the blacksmith's, the creamery and the buttermaker's house. No cars there either. He clamped his jaws and stepped into the street. As he crossed the center line, Toby leapt up and pointed up the street. "Cletus, look out, a car!"

Head down, Cletus lurched across the street for the garage door. His feet hit the wire between the benches and he fell forward through the door, the hand sickle still tight in his hand. Toby undid the wire and threw the loose end into the weeds.

"D-darn it," Cletus spluttered. He picked himself up and looked at his knuckles that had been scraped across the concrete floor. He turned and kicked at a loose pebble in the doorway.

"Why'd you s-say that, Toby, there's no car."

Toby ran his hand through his slick black hair. "But I thought I heard one, Cletus." He looked down the street as a car came into view at the head of the village. Toby recognized the car. It was Benedict Lendler and his son Bobby. "Here it comes now." He stepped out and made a show of waving to Bobby.

Cletus mumbled under his breath, *Ohren wie'n Esel.* Toby looked at him as if he didn't understand German.

"What'd you say, Cletus?" Cletus backed away, his sickle in front of him for protection.

"What'd he say, Danny?" Toby asked.

"He says you've got the ears of a jackass, Toby."

Toby grabbed the sickle from Cletus and chased him out the front door, slowing enough to allow Cletus to pull away from him. Danny went out the back door and walked past the weeds Cletus was to cut. He ducked through a hole in the high hedge and quietly opened the church's side door. He crept up to the choir loft and took the steeple-door key from the organist's bench where Cletus kept it.

Danny unlocked the tin-covered door. He closed it behind him and began to climb. It was dark—like not having been born yet. The steep narrow stairs, small for Cletus's shoulders, were wide enough for Danny. Fifteen, sixteen, he counted . . . now the church below seemed cool in comparison . . . twenty-seven . . . twenty-eight. He stopped and reached up for the ring on the trapdoor. The heat from the metal door reached down to him. He gave the trapdoor a gentle shove. A blinding white glare flooded the steps and Danny stood paralyzed by the shock to his eyes.

He squeezed past the bells and sat on the metal floor next to the dense grids that covered the large openings. The town lay at his feet; here no one could see him. Below him, the neat squares of land were dotted with farmsteads and windbreaks. The dark green oats made the black soil of the late-planted cornfields look even darker. What he needed, he thought, was a huge telescope, so he could see all the way down to the Gulf of Mexico or even to the Pacific Ocean. When he first heard about the ocean, he had nearly cried, because he knew he would never see it.

At the far end of village stood old Payter's farm, his long barn with the hayloft door open, revealing the dark hole of the haymow. Dewey,

Cletus's dog, was pestering the rabbits in Payter's rockpile where the road curved to the west. A crow rose from the rocks and flapped away.

Danny saw Cletus step out of the garage door to give the pebble another kick. He looked at the oily bench then sat down on the clean one. Cletus lived next door to Danny. Even though Cletus was forty-three, Danny felt they had something in common. When Danny was seven, his father had died in a car accident. Cletus's dad, Roman, had died too, killed when he fell off a windmill he'd climbed on a dare. Roman had found the pint of whiskey farmers always hide under a bundle of unshocked oats at harvest time. It was a prize to speed up the shockers who came out from town to set up the grain bundles to dry. Roman didn't pass it around but guzzled it down by himself.

Danny looked down to see Irvin talking to Cletus, pointing at the patch of weeds behind the garage. Sometimes Danny wondered about Roman's last thoughts as the ground rushed up to him. He turned and looked toward the cemetery where Roman was buried. His wife, Esther, had bought the smallest, slightly damaged tombstone the granite sheds had in stock. Danny reached out now and gave the metal grid in front of him a shake. It was solid. Danny was five when they brought in the Model T with Roman cramped in the back seat, his legs sticking out of the window. He came home with his feet up, a position, everybody joked, that he'd favored most of his life. Esther stared, dry-eyed, at the run-down heels of her husband's boots.

Esther's hatred of whiskey had lessened after Roman died and she allowed Cletus to make a few crocks of dandelion and wheat wine in the cellar. She claimed that it was drinking Roman's moonshine that had affected Cletus's brain, but Danny heard that Cletus had fallen down stairs too many times.

Danny saw Toby watching Cletus hack at the weeds behind the garage. Toby was the only other boy in town even near Danny's age. Toby had always said when he turned sixteen, he'd quit high school and go the Cities. The closer it got, though, the more he talked about the good money to be made polishing tombstones at the granite sheds in Cold Spring. Danny knew Toby wouldn't like it there; the huge cutting shed was hot and dark in summer, cold and dark in winter.

Danny took one last look at the horizon. Standing on tiptoes didn't help. You see what's in front of you. He closed the trapdoor and counted the steps of utter darkness.

Cletus and Danny sat on the back step, looking at Cletus's garden. It was mid-June and each six inch high bean plant stood an even twelve inches apart, just like Esther said. Cletus stood and plucked the tight strings on the fence. A dull hum vibrated against the boards. He liked training the pole beans to climb the strings. Sometimes he'd take a spindly stalk and tie a loose knot in it, just to see if it stayed that way. Cletus eyed the empty stretch of fence next to the horse barn. He told Danny he had planted beans there once, though his mother warned him that the oak's shade was too deep. She laughed as he waited for the shoots to climb the fence. He stared up at the shadow cast by the looming tree.

Cletus leaned back and pressed his nose to the screen door, sniffing the aroma of pork hocks and boiled potatoes. He turned to Danny.

"Smell those *Schweine-haxen,* Danny? I wonder if she'd hear me if went in there? I could eat ten of them, but I'll only get t-two."

Danny leaned back too and they both listened for a moment, but heard only the ticking of the alarm clock on the stove set for the evening Angelus bell. Cletus eased the screen door open. On tiptoe, he walked to the stove. Danny leaned back, and through the mesh of the screen door, saw Cletus lift the cover of the potatoes then open the oven door. Steam rose up and hit his face. Cletus jumped back. The oven door fell open with a clang. Cletus stood stock still. Danny heard only the ticking of the clock. Cletus smiled at Danny then knelt in front of the stove, his new shoes creaking as they bent at the toe. Cletus pulled on the oven shelf which held three pork hocks. Danny could smell the sizzling *Schwart',* the juicy meat and the rich fat. Cletus held up two fingers then pointed at his open mouth. Cletus put a finger into the drippings of fat in the pan below the hocks. He poked one of the hocks then pulled out the oven shelf all way out.

"CLETUS, *schäm. dich. doch*." Esther's staccato voice rang out in the quiet of the small kitchen. It reverberated off the shiny wooden floor, the perfect walls and ceiling, like the voice of God Almighty Himself. Cletus looked up. The oven shelf and the pork hocks tumbled to the floor.

"Shame on you. How often do I have to tell you, *Kameleskopf*? Stay out of my kitchen!" Cletus knelt on the floor, holding the welt on the back of his hand to his mouth. Esther took a plate from the cupboard and dropped one of the hocks on the plate.

"Wait, Ma, I-I just wanted to . . ."

Cletus cowered on the floor. The folds of his eyelids closed over his bulging eyes. He protected himself with his arms as she flailed at him with a dishtowel. "You want to live like a dog then you can eat like one . . ." As she turned to the back door, Danny ducked around the corner. She brought the other two hocks to the back door and threw them into Dewey's dish.

Danny was helping Toby wash his car again, the black 1950 Ford his grandfather Meinulph had given Toby for helping in the saloon. Now that he had his license, Toby complained he had no place to go. The nearby towns were all the same. If they didn't know you they wouldn't even sell you a beer, because the Stearns County sheriff was cracking down on kids drinking. The few village girls were out on farms for the summer, taking care of some farmer's twelve kids. Danny walked back to his house then remembered his mother wanted him to help her wax the classroom floors at the school where she taught and did the cleaning. He didn't feel like waxing floors. He stood and looked over the back fence.

Cletus untied Dewey, who hopped around the yard like a headless rooster. Cletus let him gnaw at his ankle, then shook him off. Cletus went into the old horse barn behind the house and squeezed past his father's Model T to get to the watering can on the work bench. He came out and filled it at the well pump and began to water. He stroked a tall bean plant with his hand and used his thumb and forefinger to measure the distance to the top of the tall fence. Cletus watered each cabbage plant, the neat rows of onions, the rows of potatoes. The smell of beef tongue simmering in onions and peppercorns drifted out of Esther's kitchen. Cletus put away the watering can and walked across the street to the garage. Danny followed.

Irvin and Toby were working on Cletus's Model T. Toby's wiry body hunched over the fender of the Model T. Irvin had put in new plugs, had even taken it out of the village and opened her up to burn out some of the carbon. Toby looked at the engine and turned to Cletus.

"So tell me, Cletus," he said, "when are we going to race?"

"I don't know." Cletus's eyes narrowed and he smiled. "Ma doesn't let me drive fast, but I b-bet I could beat you."

"You're joking, Cletus. With a Model T? Tell you what, I'll make it easy for you. You get a running start back at the ball diamond, when you pass me, I'll start from a dead stop and *still* beat you down to the curve by Payter's rock pile. How's that sound, or are you afraid to go fast?"

Cletus looked at the ground.

"You are, aren't you, C-C-CLE-TUS, *gel, GEL?"*

Cletus stood his ground. "No, I'm not, TO-BAK." He turned quickly and went into the garage. He glared back at Toby.

"You wait, I'll show you, TO-BAK."

Toby stared at his reflection in the garage window. He'd seen the James Dean movie. He lit another cigarette, stared, then recombed his hair.

Cletus started the car and floored the accelerator. He backed it out of the garage, and drove back to the shed. Dewey ran beside the car, biting at the skinny tires. Cletus's few chickens squawked as they darted out of the way. Dewey barked and tried to climb in. Cletus laughed and pulled him up onto the high seat.

Summer was half over, a boring summer of mild weather. Today seemed different. The clammy air of late July enveloped Danny as he entered the side door of the church. The Blessed Sacrament lamp to the right of the altar flickered weirdly inside the red glass. Streaks of dirty water were still drying in the side aisle where Cletus had mopped the church floors that morning. Danny had heard Father Reiter scold Cletus for leaving too much water. Cletus sounded scared: he liked his job, especially the bell ringing part. Danny took the key and opened the steeple door.

The smell of cut oats drifted through the steeple. The field next to the cemetery was dotted with shocks of grain in uneven rows. From his vantage point in the steeple, Danny watched the sky to the west turn a pale green. A gust of cold wind hit as towering anvil-shaped clouds moved in from the horizon. The wall of rain was coming fast, falling now on the cornfield to the west. Another cold blast of wind hit the steeple and the smaller bell shifted in its cradle. The white houses below turned greenish under the sick-looking sky. Hail rattled on the roof above him. Pea-sized, it bounced in the street like popcorn. Cletus dashed into the back door as Esther opened the front door to put out a dish of holy water to stop the hail. Down the street, two other doors opened with two more dishes of holy water. Then a third. Another roll of thunder sounded and Dewey raced from the doghouse into the hole in the barn door. A branch broke from the oak tree and skittered down the barn roof.

The metal grids shuddered and rain spattered the floor. Danny's foot slid on the wet tin as he made for the bell. It was dry under the bell but the wind howled like winter along its edge. A flash of lightning left a circle of darkness around his feet. The hail smashing against the side of the steeple, bounced through the grids and rattled on the tin. The clapper in the other bell dinged softly. A riveting stroke of lightning and a quick clap of crackling thunder caused Danny to lurch upwards and crash his head into the cone of the bell.

He went over his last confession, trying to remember which words Sister Mary Benedict had told him to say with his last breath. *O Lord, my God;* . . . how does it go? . . . *accept from Your hands, the* . . . something something . . . *death You shall choose to send me, with its pains and griefs.* Was that close enough? *Amen.* Seven years each time—plenary indulgence at the moment of death—did I get it right? did I?

The storm passed quickly. A smell like shotgun shells hung in the air when Danny slid out from under the bell. The backside of the storm was moving off to the east. The cornfield to the west was stripped, except for the long thin leaves that dangled along each stalk. Danny looked down the flattened maple tree next to the church. It must have been rotten at the core. Cletus was stumbling around the back yard, looking at the empty strings where his beans had been. He knelt next to his shredded cabbages, a jar of dark wine beside him.

The next morning, a breeze moved the curtains on Danny's window. A pickup door slammed nearby and the scrape of metal on metal drifted through the window. A coughing sound was followed by a high-pitched whine that stopped abruptly. From his bedroom, Danny saw Willem Lendler and two of his boys looking at the downed maple across the street. Willem looked at a manual and fiddled with a chain saw.

"Stand back, Gregor. We'll find out what this saw'll do."

Danny and Cletus stepped out of their front doors at the same time. Cletus looked at Willem then over at Danny. "What's Willem doing here?", he asked. "That's my job." He hitched up his pants and lumbered across the street.

Willem straddled the maple's trunk, cutting away the branches while Lucas and Gregor piled them up. Cletus shoved at Willem's shoulder.

"What you doing, Willem?" Cletus's mouth was at his ear. Cletus watched Willem flip a switch. The saw stopped.

"What's it look like I'm doing? Father Reiter called me last night about the tree. I've got a new saw I want to try."

"No. This is my job. I t-take care of the church grounds."

"Look, Cletus. Reiter said I could have the wood if I cut it up. You couldn't handle a big tree like this. You'd need a two-man saw for a trunk this size. Go back home, get a shirt on, and have some breakfast. We'll take care of this."

He pulled the rope and the saw came to life. Cletus reached past him and turned it off.

"I said, this is my job. I take care of the church, Willem."

"Like hell you do, Cletus. I'm a trustee of the church. You're doing a lousy job. You missed ringing Angelus again this morning. We've been covering for you long enough. Now get out of here."

Cletus turned to cross the street. He stopped as a car approached. It was Toby in his black coupe. Toby started to hiccup the car toward him, hitting the gas, then the brake, then the gas until the car rocked drunkenly on its springs. He stopped and leaned out the window as the car settled into place. He looked at Cletus then turned to Danny and raised his eyebrows. He turned back to Cletus.

"Hey, are you hot, Cletus? Where's your shirt?" He reached out and poked Cletus's white shoulder. "Looks like a good day for a race. You hot for a race, Cletus? When you're ready, come down and get me." He rolled the car forward. "No excuses."

Toby left two streaks of rubber in a cloud of blue smoke. Cletus jumped as a patch of damp sand pelted his bare feet. The front door opened. Esther clutched her long nightgown to her skinny chest. "Cletus, *bista ganz übergeschnappt?*" Are you crazy? What are doing outside like that? Go upstairs and get dressed."

Cletus and Danny watched the chickens scratch in the damp soil of the garden. The shattered leaves of the cabbages were already curled and brown at the edges. He pulled on his second jar of dark wheat wine. He turned to Danny. "That *arsch-loch* thinks I can't cut a tree? I don't need a fancy saw to do my work." He glowered up at the crown of the tree, at the good light caught on the leaves far above the ground along the fence. The front door slammed as Esther was leaving with her grocery bags.

Cletus hid the jar, then pulled it out again when she was safely gone. "Damn Willem, he never worked in the busch like I did, freezing my ass cutting wood for fifty cents a day. Can't cut that big a tree with a hand saw? That's how much he knows, Danny. I could cut it with a buck-saw if I had to." He took another drink from the jar. "Damn oak, making me look stupid, her laughing at me all the time."

Cletus placed the jar on the overturned wheelbarrow and walked into the shed. He came out with a rusted bucksaw and started to notch the tree. "I'll show him, Danny. I've got my own tree. I'll just drop it right here and show him how fast I cut it up. I don't care if he is a trustee of the church."

Cletus sawed furiously at the tree. He was already sweating, his shirt dark along the straps of his overalls.

"What's your hurry, Cletus?" Danny asked.

"Show Willem, that's what I'm doing." He unsnapped his overalls, pulled off his shirt and threw it against the barn door. "I Like Ike" landed smile up in a halo of greasy fingerprints. Cletus's doughy white skin shone in the sun.

"Aren't you afraid of hitting the barn, Cletus? There's not much room back here."

"That's what you know about it, Danny. I've seen guys drive a stake into the ground by d-dropping a tree on it. I worked with the old-timers." He pushed back the bill of his cap.

In ten more minutes, he'd taken wedges out of the tree as deep as the buck-saw would go. He went into the shed and brought out a shiny double-bit axe. "Watch it now. This is what I'm good at." The chips flew past his ears and over his shoulder with every grunt. He growled at the tree, as spit leaked from the side of his mouth. A drop of sweat hung from his nose.

"Come on down, you bastard," he yelled. He pulled at the wine, then ran to look down the street. The tree was starting to shiver now. Cletus was on the backside of the tree, avoiding the wall of the barn with a shortened swing.

"Hey, Cletus, it's starting to twist. Better come over here."

"I don't need you to tell me how to cut trees, Danny." He switched to the other half of the double bit again. "Damn thing's getting dull," he puffed. Sweat streamed from his short hair, shreds of wood hung from his face. The oak creaked, shivered again, then twisted. Cletus ran to the other side, trying to deepen the notch. The branches shuddered. The tree followed the weight of the heaviest branch and crashed through the roof of the house.

"*Ver-DAMMT noch a mal.*" Cletus's mouth stood agape. He threw the axe to the ground. He held his head, "What am I going to d-do now?" He looked in the direction of the grocery store. *"Mein Gott."* He lumbered to the front of the house and looked down the road. His eyes bulged below his heavy forehead. Danny ran back to his house and sat on the steps as if nothing had happened.

He heard Cletus fire up the car and saw him drive down past the saloons toward Toby's house. Danny wandered over to the hedge and slipped into the side door of the church. He blinked as he remembered how afraid he had been just yesterday; but it was safe now. He climbed the stairs. The horizon seemed closer, like the world was getting smaller. From the steeple the huge hole in Esther's roof looked into an upstairs bedroom. The trunk had collapsed one wall of the room. He looked down and saw Esther was marching along the side of the street as if her bulging bags weighed nothing. Cletus drove by her, hunched over—as if she couldn't see him. He stopped in front of Toby's house.

Danny heard a car door slam. Toby's coupe, low, black and shiny, followed Cletus's high boxy Model T up the street. Irvin looked up from the gas pump to watch them pass. Now they were below the steeple. The Ford pulled to the side of the road and the Model T continued down to the crossroad a quarter mile away. Toby made a U turn and got into the left lane. He got out, waved and jumped back in. His engine roared, followed by a scream from Esther that pierced the air.

Esther's head turned from the tree, to the house, back to the tree again. She ran around the barn, yelling for Cletus. Toby's engine roared again. She ran to the street. Cletus, a dark shadow behind the wheel, raced down the tar. Toby lit a cigarette and watched his side mirror to gauge when Cletus would be even with him.

Cletus was doing forty-five by the time he passed the low black coupe. A roar went up from the road and Toby missed a gear in his fever to catch up. Cletus saw Esther, her fist upraised. Gathering speed, he swerved towards his mother. A scream contorted her twisted face as she jumped back from the road.

Cletus shot past Irvin, racing toward Kellner's saloon. Toby was gaining fast, in high gear in the left lane. Cletus was doing fifty-five. The spokes in the front wheels were an invisible blur. Toby gained as they passed the creamery. He was pulling ahead as they approached the curve on the north end of village. Toby began to pass as Dewey looked up from the rock pile. The dog ran toward the Model T, leaping into the road just as Cletus entered the curve. Cletus veered off to avoid hitting Dewey. The Model T swerved back to the ditch and flipped end over end, landing upside down on Payter's rock pile, crushing Cletus's body. A crow flapped up, circled slowly toward Payter's barn and the open hayloft and its black form disappeared before the gaping black hole.

Below the Surface

In the mid-fifties, the government started handing out money to all comers to put more farmland into production. My Uncle Benedict decided pasturing was a waste of land and old fashioned. A dairy feedlot would be the wave of the future. Having the government pay to pull a main ditch and install grass waterways looked like money in the bank. He signed the papers and the government sent out a surveyor with a plan to straighten and deepen the crick, drain ten acres of swamp, and pick up the flow from the watershed to the west. It was a big change, but just the beginning of a lot of changes we'd go through that year.

My uncle had twisted his back that spring, so my dad offered to send me over to clear the land, some sixty acres of low, rocky pasture and swamp. My uncle's seventeen-year-old son, Bobby, was going to work with me. We're cousins but I didn't know Bobby that well, him being four years younger. We're all cousins here, intermarried so often and in so many ways, nobody can keep us straight. I had seen him at the Friday night dances in Spring Hill for a number of years.

Spring Hill was wide open then—if you were tall enough to get your money on the bar you could drink until you were drunk. People drank a lot, and said and did things they normally wouldn't. Getting drunk set you free; sober, there was a line to toe.

Huge crowds of kids came from other towns, parking and double-parking beyond the creamery, stumbling and puking past the church and out to the blacktop. Meinulph shut down the cash register and put out galvanized buckets for the extra bartenders to throw all the money into, especially on nights when a polka band like the Six Fat Dutchmen played.

The out-of-town kids paid the forty cents at the dance hall for a ticket to drink and stare, like we were some kind of show they could watch.

Bobby and I started work on a Saturday morning, slightly hung over. We decided to cut the trees first, a stand of white oak in a small grove. From the start we got on well because we both liked working hard and fast. Sometimes, being a few years older, I felt I ought to rein him in a bit because he could get reckless. He had a natural way of working, though, like someone twice his age. He'd never used a two-man saw before but he had the knack for it. The trick to the two-man is to pull then relax, pull then relax. Pushing causes it to bind in the saw-path. Bobby was good at it, even with Brutus, his fourteen-year-old black lab, nipping at his elbow on the pull-stroke. Cutting and towing the trees took only a few days; the stumps we left for the bulldozer to grub out.

As we worked, Brutus chased cars on the road, a bad habit farm dogs have. We had just hooked onto a tree trunk when we heard a yelp from the long dust plume a feed truck was raising on the gravel road. When the dust lifted, Brutus was lying on the gravel, craning his black head up as if to see what had happened. The dual wheels had caught his rear legs, crushing his hip bones like an empty paper bag. I warned Bobby away, thinking that Brutus might strike out at him. I was wrong. Brutus licked Bobby's hand. I could hardly watch; they'd spent their whole lives together.

Swallowing a bit, I told Bobby I would put Brutus out of his misery. Bobby shook his head, walked back to our tools, and picked up a shovel. With a quick blow to the head, Bobby ended Brutus's life. He picked Brutus up and carried him across the ditch to a shallow depression near the road. We buried him there without a word. When we finished, Bobby laid the shovel next to the other tools, carefully, so all the handles lined up. He glanced at the horizon for a second, half-turned toward the sun and said, "Ten-thirty. Let's get going." He'd had Brutus since he was three years old.

When I was eight my Aunt Suzanna died. My sister Eva and I started crying at her funeral and we couldn't stop. I remembered the uneasy looks we got from relatives, all dry-eyed, as if there were something wrong with us for crying at all. By the time we got control of ourselves, I couldn't tell if I was crying for Aunt Suzanna or out of shame for my own tears.

◇

We finished with the trees and began grubbing out the rocks. We had a John Deere B, three log chains, a flat stone-boat, a crow bar, a grub ax, two pointy shovels and our bare hands. The bulldozer operator was coming in four weeks to bury the rocks before the earth movers came to shape the land for the grass waterways. The crane of the drag line was visible half a mile away, working its way along Uncle Karl's part of the crick. It was leaving piles of dirt in a long row like a tidy pocket gopher.

As we worked, our eyes kept going to a huge red rock by the road. It had a foot-deep trench around it and measured eight-foot-some across. Dead center of it was a hand-drilled hole about a foot deep where someone had failed to split the rock with dynamite. Uncle Benedict told us that it would be impossible for us to remove the rock. On days when things were going badly we agreed with him; when things were going well, we saw it as a challenge from the quitters who'd drilled the hole and dug the trench around the rock. We had no idea how much of the rock lay below the surface.

We started small, pulling out pointy rocks that stuck a couple of feet above the ground. We would position the flat wooden stone-boat in front of a rock and pop it onto the boat with the tractor and log chains, hoping to haul it away without having to handle it twice. In a few days the two of us had developed a routine. Bobby, who used to be on the short side, had grown five inches in the last year. In the course of a few weeks of hard labor he was turning into a muscle man. Aunt Philomena claimed we were eating for four.

When the drag line moved through the line fence to Uncle Benedict's pasture, we had a rock pile ninety feet long and ten feet wide. The red rock grew smaller as we got stronger and more skilled. Even the deepest, most oddly shaped rock didn't stand a chance against us. Bobby and I would dig from opposite sides, trenching enough to slip a chain under the bulk of the rock then using sheer muscle and a gradual increase of tension on the chain to loosen the earth's grip.

One day the wind died and it was so hot and humid that our heavy sweat-soaked jeans almost pulled right off our bodies as we worked.

When we drove home for dinner at noon, we agreed that the big red rock would be next. Uncle Benedict had finished cultivating corn and was at an auction in Lake Henry. When he came home we wanted to surprise him with what we'd done.

I began trenching the backside of the red rock as Bobby dug a ramp to free the front so that the rock would slide smoothly out of its hole. We worked fast, the sweat running down our bare backs. The volume of dirt we had to move was staggering.

Finally I was able to snug the chain around the rock slightly below what I took to be the thickest part, where it began to curve back under, like we had done a hundred times before. I was holding the point of my shovel on the chain to keep it from riding up, the rock being very smooth. As Bobby climbed onto the tractor seat, he must have bumped the hand clutch, because the tractor leapt forward. The chain tightened, caught, then slid off the rock and zinged through the air like a cracked whip. In a split second Bobby lay draped over the axle like half a sack of oats. The tractor stopped the instant he fell. I ran up to him. The pupils of his eyes had rolled up to where I couldn't see them. The chain had hit the side of his head as he was looking back at me. I screamed in his ear but there was no sign he could hear me. Above his ear his head was swelling.

I put him on the stone boat but then thought it might bounce him too much, so I lifted him back up on the tractor seat. He was quite a handful for me. I held him in front of me and drove back to the house with him slumped over, his head jouncing around as if he were dead. I had to drive with one hand, holding my other hand under his chin and pressing his head to my chest.

Aunt Philomena was in the potato patch and I yelled to her. We were taking Bobby down when my uncle came home. He called Doctor Gans, who said to bring him in but to put ice on the bruise which now was the size of an orange. My aunt and uncle were taking it all more calmly than I was, considering Bobby was their only son.

The whole fifteen miles to the hospital in Paynesville I could feel my heart pound in my chest. When Doctor Gans examined Bobby, I could tell he was worried that Bobby was still unconscious. They x-rayed his head and then put him in a quiet room. My aunt and uncle and I sat there in those soft chairs and looked at Bobby, feeling completely helpless. I couldn't stop explaining how it happened. It was my fault, being older, that I hadn't slowed the pace and I told Uncle Benedict and Aunt Philomena as much. I looked into their faces for some sign of how they were taking it. My uncle's glasses kept sliding down his nose, and he sat, then stood and walked, blaming the soft chairs for his sore back. I think he didn't want to let on how worried he was, his only son laid out there on the hospital bed that was looking more and more like a coffin. Aunt Philomena's hand kept moving back to a missing button on her print dress, as if she were ashamed to be wearing her work dress in town.

Bobby's eyes started zigzagging back and forth and his brow wrinkled. He let out a moan. His hand went right up to the ice bag they'd attached to the side of his head. My uncle pushed the nurse's button and Bobby's eyes opened.

Aunt Philomena was standing over him and Bobby gave her the most beautiful smile, as if he'd been gone a year. He reached up and took her into his arms and kissed her full on the lips. Aunt Philomena cried and he kissed her again, tears streaming down his face. By now she was pulling back a bit and looking over her shoulder at us. I doubt whether Bobby had kissed her once since he was three years old. Uncle Benedict moved to her side and suddenly Bobby had his arm around his dad's shoulder. When Bobby kissed him too, he stiffened up like a two by four.

The nurse came in and I almost expected him to kiss her too. His color had come back from pale and he was brown as a kernel of wheat from all the sun. He still had dirt on his chest from grubbing rock. He was breathing easier. I was hoping he could come home with us, feeling more than a little responsible for all the trouble (not that Uncle Benedict couldn't handle the expense). Doctor Gans decided to keep him overnight and put him on a clear liquid diet, so that he wouldn't vomit.

We had chores to do and Aunt Philomena had the other kids to feed. It was an awkward moment when we went over to the bed. Bobby grabbed his mother and kissed her and it was all Uncle Benedict could do to keep from getting kissed again. Bobby was content to shake my hand, but he brought his other hand over from the other side of the bed and he held onto me with both hands for what felt like an eternity. This was not the dry-eyed Bobby who had buried Brutus.

On the way home I offered to help pay the bill, but they wouldn't hear of it. In fact, Uncle Benedict said, he'd been thinking of giving us a bonus for working so fast. As we drove down Highway 4 there was a little silence until Uncle Benedict looked in the rear-view mirror and asked me, "*Ja, dann, was meinsta davon?*"

"What do I think about what?" I asked.

Uncle Benedict looked a little peeved at me. "About Bobby's condition," he said with a snort.

"He looked fine to me," I said, "considering he'd been hit on the side of the head with a chain."

Uncle Benedict leveled another look back at me in the mirror. "I mean," he said, "about when we were leaving."

In the mirror I could see the worried look on his face. I told him maybe it was the concussion that had made him so wild and that a good night's sleep would get him back to his old self. I did volunteer that he acted a bit bright-eyed and bushy-tailed for someone who'd had a serious blow to the head. Bobby looked a bit *too* alive but at least, thank God, he wasn't dead.

We took a few days off, even though the doctor told Bobby he could go home and not to use this as an excuse to get out of work, because he was fine. On Friday we were back at it, grubbing smaller rocks and ignoring the mounds of dirt around the red rock. Uncle Benedict told us to slow down. He needn't have bothered. From the start, there was something different about Bobby. He kept going on about how beautiful a morning it was and would you look at the color of that cloud. Even the long-legged schlough-pomper croaking in the swamp interested him for the first time. A butterfly went skimming by, yellow with black markings, and he was off chasing it through the pasture like he'd gone off his head. When he came back, wet up to the knees from what was left of the swamp, I knew Bobby was a changed man. That night I was as tired as I'd ever been on our fastest hottest days.

Our cousin Laura's wedding was the next day. She was getting married to my cousin Harold, a cousin from my mother's side. Bobby and I decided, since we were invited from both sides, so to speak, that we'd take the whole day off. That night I was still so put out about Bobby that I didn't feel like going to the dance. The next morning, I helped with the milking, without a hangover for a change. After breakfast I decided I'd go to the wedding Mass with my folks, Laura being, after all, a closer cousin because I'd been at school with her. A little ahead of us, on the other side of the aisle, I saw Bobby and his folks. Bobby was taking in the sights of the church as if he'd never been there before, twisting his neck this way and that to look at the summer light streaming through the stained glass and then over toward the little gold stars floating in the blue plaster sky above the Blessed Virgin's head. Uncle Benedict shifted in the pew and Aunt Philomena, blushing a little, stared down at her lap. Even Romuald and Reiner unrolling the white cloth down the center aisle lit up his eyes. His face was too open for someone his age. Every thought registered on it, like a gust of wind crossing a barley field.

Toby, the new bellringer who took Cletus's job, started ringing the bell and Father Reiter came to the altar. There was the usual bustle behind us and everyone turned to see the bride. Bobby, eyes half-filled with shiny tears, was completely taken with what he was seeing. His eyes darted around the church and Bobby just glowed, like a light bulb that burns a little too bright just before it gives out.

Bobby got some odd looks from the people right behind him, including old Onkel Payter who leaned on his cane and stared straight at Bobby as if he were some new sort of *Dummkopf.* I have to admit Laura was the most beautiful bride I'd ever seen too, although I didn't go on and on about it in the reception line or give any long lingering kisses like someone I needn't even mention who.

Girls hung around Bobby in threes and fours, like a new blossom bees couldn't get enough of. I was happy for him but couldn't imagine what his life would be like here if he couldn't get a hold of himself.

Everyone went back to church basement for supper. I got stuck going home to do the milking. As I moved from cow to cow, I wasn't thinking about the log chain snaking out at him so much as recalling the picture of Aunt Philomena as she pulled back from Bobby and looked over her shoulder at me and Uncle Benedict with that odd mixture of love and disgust. A part of me didn't want to believe that expression, but I realized Bobby's parents were no different from anyone else.

That night things got worse. Bobby danced with Laura again and again while Harold downed big whiskey sours until he was scarlet around the eyes. His fist clenched and unclenched over this pup cousin who was horning in on his wedding day. Finally Laura's dad, Martin, tapped Bobby on the shoulder with his hook arm and told him to quit it. I stumbled home at one that morning, having seen about all I could stand. I wanted to sit down on my bed and cry. Then I started worrying that what Bobby had, I might have caught too.

Bobby and I had suffered a setback but we still had the deadline. I drove by the big red rock in silence, not giving it a glance. Bobby didn't notice it either, gassing on and on about the sunrise like it was the first one he'd ever seen. We started to work, thinking about the deadline, knowing we had to bull our way through the job. We went at it with all the enthusiasm of an artificial inseminator. When Uncle Benedict came out to check on our progress, he talked to me as if Bobby weren't even there.

On Wednesday I came to pick Bobby up and he was all excited about a book he'd found in the attic, a book about butterflies. It had a picture of the very butterfly he'd seen. A tiger swallowtail, he said, like he'd discovered something important, like the man in the moon was really a woman.

When we finished the job, on time, Bobby and I went out to watch the bulldozer take out the big red rock. With one side exposed, it was as high as our heads and more than the smoke-belching D7 could handle. We didn't know it at the time but we hadn't had a chance. It was so big the operator decided to leave it. He deepened the hole next to it and buried it even deeper.

Bobby never missed a dance now at the dance hall in Spring Hill. One night, I saw him, a Grain Belt in hand, watching as two boys we didn't know were laughing at two local girls dancing together. He was taking it all in with those wide-set eyes and that long nose that marked him as one of us. The boys, a little drunk, danced a few feet apart, swooping and pumping their long arms, making fun of the girls. Bobby had a shocked look on his face, as if he had seen some beautiful thing savaged. It took three of us to drag him out of the scuffle that followed.

At the end of July, Father Reiter went fishing in Canada so he invited a touring priest from the missions in Mississippi to say Mass and preach. Bobby was sitting a few rows ahead of me when the priest, a tall, rugged-looking man, came to the podium to read the Epistle. As he fiddled with Father Reiter's new PA system, the church echoed with squawking, whistling sounds that caused Bobby to cover his ears.

When the priest got the PA to work, he read the Epistle in a sing-songy voice that *made* me to listen more closely than ususal. It was Paul's letter to the Corinthians about the varieties of gifts but the same Spirit, the varieties of ministries but the same Lord, the varieties of workings but the same God, who works in all things. Bobby had settled down and cocked his head to the side, as if he were listening closely too. The priest read the Gospel in the same voice, about the Pharisee thanking God he was not like the publican at the back of the temple praying, God be merciful to me, the sinner.

After the Gospel, the missionary talked about the missions in the South. He began to complain how the Seventh Day Adventists were competing for conversions and what hypocrites they were, spreading rumors about Catholics. Bobby stared as the priest got more and more worked up. The priest's voice boomed out of the wall speaker that the Adventists were evil and preached a false Gospel. Bobby squirmed in his seat, turning sideways to look at the faces around him. Suddenly he got up and marched up toward the altar. He went around the communion rail and stood in front of the priest. The priest stared at Bobby, not knowing what to make of him coming up. Bobby said, "Didn't you just read that there are different kinds of ministries and he who exalts himself shall be humbled and he who humbles himself shall be exalted?"

"Yes, but sit down. You don't belong up here. Go back to your seat." The priest ran his hand through his silver hair. Bobby went around the podium.

"Then why are you complaining about these other missionaries? Don't they believe in the Gospel and Jesus too? Or weren't you listening to what you read?" Whispering, murmuring, even a few small laughs began to fill the church.

The priest's voice squawked over the PA system, "Sit down, you can't be up here. Go back to your seat."

Bobby moved to cover his ears but then he pulled the microphone off the priest's chest. We'd all been taught to not even whisper in the church.

"Give me that," the priest yelled.

"You're the hypocrite. Father Reiter doesn't talk like this."

The priest reached for the microphone and Bobby pushed him and the priest *fell.* One of the trustees of the church ran to the front, and motioned to Reiner and Romuald. When they walked by with Bobby between them, I expected him to look crazy but he didn't. He looked like he knew exactly what he was doing.

Everybody from miles around was talking now. Attacking a priest—nothing could be worse than that. There was no telling what he'd do next. He might even murder someone. There was no way anyone would ever forget this. There was talk about having him locked up in Fergus. Bobby ignored it all. I wondered if he even knew what was being said behind his back. To his face, everybody acted like it never happened. About this time a bad imitation of Bobby could get a cheap laugh anywhere. People I hardly recognized asked me about him. It was the accident, I told them, the accident made him do it.

At the beginning of August, the posters went up for the first rock and roll band the saloon keepers ever hired from the Cities. That Friday night, I wondered if there was one under-age kid within fifty miles who hadn't shown up for a share of beer and rock and roll. I got there early and I was in Meinulph's saloon across the street from the dance hall with my cousins Gregor and Lucas. The jukebox was going as usual but not with the old polkas and waltzes or even Vic Damone. It was Johnny Ray choking out "The Little White Cloud that Cried," Bill Haley and the Comets, and both the Carl Perkins and Elvis Presley versions of "Blue Suede Shoes" played over and over again.

Looking out of the front window, we could see no end to the stream of kids coming down the street, a good number of duck-tail haircuts mixed in with the occasional familiar face walking into the light from the beer sign.

Suddenly, into that light came Bobby. He saw us and came over to pound on the window with a big smile on his face. He lifted his foot and pointed down at it. We couldn't see what he was pointing at so we motioned him to come inside. His face was shining with sweat as he pushed his way through the crowd toward us. Again he pointed down at his feet and shouted, "BLUE SUEDE SHOES." He started to dance in front of us and the three of us half-turned away from him, thinking maybe he was expecting us to dance right there.

He was excited by the size of the crowd and we talked for a few minutes, him so close you could almost feel his breath, there not being any room to back away. I was glad when he saw one of his new girlfriends outside and he pushed his way back out to be with her. It was noisy and smoky, the floor wet from spilled beer. A kid in a duck-ass haircut was throwing up along the fence that separated the dance hall from the cow pasture that ran right up to the main street of Spring Hill.

The noise in the saloon got louder and louder. Gregor, Lucas and I got some beers and waded through the crowd into the street. The dance hall was packed. We looked in through the upraised flaps of the hall at what looked like a many-footed, many-headed animal pulsing in darkness. Screams, laughs and the smell of sweat and beer gusted out of the big flaps on the heavy rock and roll beat. It didn't feel like our town anymore.

Gregor had a pint and we sat outside to cool off and watch the crowd. When we finished the whiskey at about midnight we saw Bobby, handsome as ever, this time between two girls we didn't know but could appreciate, an arm draped around each of them. They were looking down at his blue suede shoes and trying to march in step, kicking empty beer bottles as they came. He saw us and turned up the palms of his hands, never taking his arms from their shoulders, as if to say, here I am, look at me. They turned the corner into the darkness behind the dance hall. Not a minute later three guys followed them, their greasy hair shining under the street light.

Over the noise from the dance hall we heard a long scream. When we ran behind the dance hall, the three of them were going after Bobby, one holding, two hitting with their fists. We rushed up to fight them and they ran, but not before the holding one clubbed Bobby with something heavy. The girls vanished like they do and we carried Bobby back to the street light. It was like last June all over again. I turned my face, glad for the music and darkness that covered my tears. We loaded him into Gregor's car and took him home. By the time we woke up Aunt Philomena and Uncle Benedict, Bobby was awake, a big headache already in progress. He lay there on the davenport, not hugging or kissing anybody.

The next morning he was fine, but a day later I knew there was something wrong with him. He'd get this vacant look on his face and he didn't even recognize his own gloves. His sister Rosalie quietly asked me if I thought Bobby was retarded. I told her I didn't know. She and I finally convinced his parents to take him in for a checkup. Doctor Gans wasn't sure but thought Bobby might have had some kind of closed head injury.

Everybody said Bobby was fine now, that it was a phase he'd gone through. He fit in a lot better too, as if the second hit had flipped a switch back to off. I knew things didn't work that way. I was sure he'd never be his old self again.

In September, when I was returning my uncle's silage wagon with the pickup, Aunt Philomena was digging the last of the year's potatoes. It was muddy and she was wearing Bobby's blue suede shoes, as if not to ruin her own. I asked her about Bobby and she said he and my uncle were nearly finished breaking sod on the new sixty acres we'd cleared. She looked at me with such a sad expression, I was tempted to go over to hug her but I was afraid she might not understand what I meant.

I drove west on the gravel road and crossed what used to be the crooked little crick. The rain from the night before had all but drained completely away, down the new ditch that lay across the land as straight as the ruler the surveyor had used to draw it. At the far end of the field Bobby and Uncle Benedict were plowing the last furrow, Bobby's tractor following my uncle's.

The newly-plowed field lay smooth and bare under the gray fall sky. The long rock pile Bobby and I had worked so hard to gather had been buried. There was no sign of the long-legged schlough-pomper because there was no longer any sign of the swamp. I thought I would remember where the red rock had been, but I wasn't sure. It was still there, of course, but it was buried without a trace. Brutus's grave had disappeared under the plow too. The old Bobby from last spring was gone and so was the Blue Suede Bobby who attacked a hypocrite one Sunday when no one expected it. I couldn't imagine it would be too long before I was gone too.

There is a Name for This

That morning I argue with my mother. It starts small: there are so many of us, the house is so loud, everyone at the table always watching the plates like there won't be enough. It goes on from there. I don't mean it. It just comes out: quit having so many kids. Is that all you can do with your life?

Her eyes go wide and she looks down the table at all our faces. She knows it's not a real question. She stares at my father, then down at her plate. Her face, still a little pink from planting potatoes the day before, sags a bit and her hand touches her fork lightly. For once, no one is talking. Just wait until you're older she says quietly. Then: that dress is too tight.

It's so loud.

Sometimes I want to holler "*RUH-IG*" like my father when he wants quiet, and then it is quiet. The clock ticks and the fire hisses in the cookstove and in my ears. But it doesn't work for me. Or rap on the window like he does in summer from the couch on the porch and there isn't another sound until we hear him snoring, schnarchsing, and then there is a whisper then two or three until the house is loud again then "*PASS AUF*," a warning, look out. It doesn't work for me.

I'm packing the lunches, five syrup pails all lined up. Each lid is marked with nail holes in the shape of our initials. The lunches are all the same: butterbread, apple, egg, a paper-twist of salt.

My brother goes to the barn. Gregor is fourteen, grown up and finished with school. Finally the rest are off, swinging their pails. I'll catch up. Sweep first, dishes, make beds, then run. Two miles and some by road, less if I cut through the pastures; the crick is almost low enough. There are snakes down there. Once my sister picked one up by the tail and swung it and it bit her high on the leg. She bled.

My mother is looking after the chickens. My father drives by on the tractor with a load of bales. The fire hisses in the stove. Something is wrong. It is quiet. I check to see if the babies are breathing. They are. I want to sit on the floor and rest. There isn't time. I still see her hand on the fork. I want to make it up to her.

My shoes are just a little wet.

I cut through the sheep pasture even though my Uncle Jerome's schafbuck is there, standing off by himself away from the ewes. He's facing east, looking into the wind. It is so quiet I think I can hear the breeze whistle in his big horns. I want to sit on the springy grass and rest. There isn't time.

I hear the school handbell and the honk-squawk of the pump. I see my little brother carrying water into school from the well. It's not a punishment. The boys take turns. I'm going to be late. I stop at the girls' *beck haus* before I go in. It's dark and smelly. Before I sit down I look down the hole at my sister's good mittens. She put the mittens between her hinder and the cold seat last winter and they fell in. There's no paper.

It's hot inside the school. Mrs. Cabot is always cold. Shelves of syrup pails sit behind the stove. Three of my cousins are missing today because their mom died. Almost all of us kids are related.

I like school. It's quiet. She's not much of a teacher but she keeps good order. *Alles in Ordnung.* A place for everything and everything . . .

Easter is late this year. Drawings of pink-eared bunnies and yellow chicks cover the north windows. The south windows we need for light. Sweat trickles down my back. I close my eyes. Just for a second. My head jerks back up. Mrs. Cabot stares at me but doesn't speak. It's hot but quiet. The fire hisses in the stove.

We're going to the wake after school. My brother comes with the car to take us. It's only quarter of a mile. The whole school is going. Everyone laughs and we pile in. Next year, Gregor will get his license.

It's a '51 Nash. We've got three rows deep in the back seat. Four across. That's twelve kids. Six in the front seat. Makes eighteen. Both first-graders lie on the ledge of the back window. Twenty. Laughing and punches. Two left standing. They go to the trunk. Gregor says no, it's not safe. So one sits on the floor between his legs, the other on his left between my brother and his door. The teacher stands on the steps. I know that look. She's glad she's not from here.

It's so loud.

We drive into the yard. We're the only car. Everyone else is in the fields. We pile out and it's quiet, the middle of the afternoon. My cousins who missed school have their Sunday clothes on. They look at us like strangers. Their aunt from their mother's side holds their new brother who is only three days old. We crowd around the coffin and stare. She looks like she's resting, her eyes closed for just for a second. They've made her face look pink. A clock ticks somewhere.

The baby cries and the aunt leaves and it's just us school kids and my brother and a three- and four-year-old. It makes me nervous. Gregor says maybe we should kneel and someone should start the rosary. The aunt looks in. She's holding a baby bottle. She has a sad smile for us and prays along standing in the door. I think we're related too but can't remember how.

The baby cries from upstairs and the aunt leaves again. The four-year-old pulls a chair to the coffin. He says wake up, Mama, talk. We're all staring at him, like we're mentals from Fergus. He starts to crawl into the coffin and his little sister tries to climb the chair too. We're praying but it straggles off and everybody looks down or over at the empty door for help. I'm in the back. I look at Gregor. His face is blank.

He's supposed to be older.

I jump up, but before I get there the boy is in the coffin, moving her mouth. I touch his shoulder lightly. He looks back at me, as if I've come to help. His hand bunches her Sunday dress. I take him out and straighten the dress with my free hand. He's crying and reaching for his mother and his sister is hanging on my leg. One of my tears lands on his head and he puts his hand up and feels his hair then looks at me but he doesn't know me, even though we're related. He tries to turn and hit at me but I hold him and sway a little. He stops kicking and stares and I sway some more. His body goes loose and I peer around at his face and his eyes are going shut then open. His sister's fingernails cut into my stockings. I'd forgotten about her.

We pray the Sorrowful Mysteries, then we pack up the Nash. Some of the kids to the north walk home so it isn't so crowded. When we get home, the noise starts all over again. I help my mother with supper. I don't care how loud it gets.

I Will Fall into Barley

For a day now, a small brown heifer has failed to deliver the calf that swells her body to bursting. Her waters are broken; the calf is too large. She has not eaten. I am to keep her moving, not allow her to stay down too long. She sees me coming. If an animal can sigh, this one seems to. I lean over the curve of the concrete manger and look down at her. The dim lightbulb above me shimmers in the liquid of her eyes.

Steh auf I say. She looks away, and the curve of her neck ripples with light. She does not get up. I tap her nose then tug at her ear. As she swings her head away from me, the metal eartag slashes my hand. My blood oozes a slow red. She stands mute, anchored from within by the size of her calf. I leave the barn and head for the field, marching myself through the damp stillness of late fall. Deep inside my head, my ear aches from yesterday's wind.

A hanging mist advances and retreats before the horizon that is uncomfortably close. The trees have given up their leaves. Bare branches reach up into the wet fog. I walk along the standing water that fills the long muddy ruts in the lane. I look down. The trees overhead are reflected in the water at my feet. Hesitantly I lean forward and see myself, suspended in the trees, above the oily surface of the water. I hurry to the potato field, alone. The frostbitten leaves of the potato plants dangle from blackened stalks. The field lies flattened, as if trampled by animals. There is no sign of life.

I go to the long wagon to get the bushel basket and walk to the first row, the empty basket bumping my leg. Bending over the scattered potatoes, I fill the bushel basket three quarters-full, almost more than I can carry, and walk back to the wagon. My right glove has holes, *Daume und*

Zeige-finger: thumb and index, like all old gloves. My left hand is warm. I heave the basket onto the wagon pole. The rope handles tighten and dig into the palms of my hands. The lip of the heavy basket catches the edge of the wagon, slides to the left and a few potatoes bounce on the wooden floor. The basket teeters and some potatoes fall to the ground. I push against its flat bottom. It empties. I retrieve the fallen potatoes. The frayed bill of my cap twists to the side. I straighten it and with the dry insides of my wrists, I tug the flaps down over my ears. The flaps never quite cover the earlobe. My breath comes in quick gray puffs that blend into the horizon. My boots pull heavily at my feet. To a passing bird, I am of no interest.

The weightless rain hangs in the air, fuzzels of water too light to fall all the way to the ground but dense enough to give shape to the movement of air that lifts over a slight rise then falls on the plot of ground where I work. Walking back from the wagon, I ball up my right hand into a fist to warm it. The empty fingers of the glove flap as I walk. *Daume, Zeigefinger, lange Mathis, Dippe-lecker, leise-Knäcker.* Thumb, forefinger, tall Mathis, pot-licker, crack-softer: the words run through my head.

I walk back to the long rows of potatoes my mother dug while I was at school. As I work, I see her tracks. Digging the first stack of potatoes, her shoes are still clean and leave a clear print. As she works, her footprints grow longer and wider. Five rectangular holes mark the spot where she drove the tines of the fork into the ground and cleaned her shoes on its horizontal metal bar. Dim light glistens off the shiny curls of mud scraped from her shoes . . . *Dippe-lecker, leise-Knäcker, Daume* . . . now her footprints are smaller but their edges remain ragged. There's no one here but me. I switch my gloves and my right hand begins to warm. My fingers struggle against the backwards gloves. I glance at where the sun would be setting. It is hard to believe the sun is there, somewhere behind the gray wall of the sky. There is time for one more row. . . *leise-Knäcker, Daume, Zeigefinger, lange Mathis* . . . my stiff lips hardly move. Shadows fall everywhere. I finish the row and put the basket under the wagon, hoping I've done enough.

I walk home past the busch where the winter wood waits in great heaps to be cut to stove length. There are jumbled piles of old lumber from buildings we salvaged in town last summer. Under a shade tree that is bare now, the sawbucks still stand where my sisters and I pulled old rusted nails and straightened them to be reused. Next to them, half-hidden by rattling milkweed, are long pole-like maples. We cut them from my grandfather's woodlot last winter. The woodlot where Aunt Suzanna hanged herself.

I remember how my grandfather stiefeled through snow banks in his six-buckle overshoes, his long sheepskin *pelz* leaving a faint track in the glittering frost. With an axe held like a hatchet, my grandfather leaves an angry slash on each tree to be taken. Sometimes he has to look up. It is then that I want to ask him which tree it was. I dare not. I want to ask will it happen to me. I cannot.

A gull flies north, lost.

I round the corner of the busch. The sound of the tractor fills the yard with the relentless whir of the hammer mill grinding feed. The tractor stands as if tethered to the granary by the wide leather belt that drives the hammer mill grinder. A dark looping track of belt dressing keeps the belt from slipping on the tractor's pully wheel. I am dizzied by the wavering line and look away.

Pressing my back to the open door, I watch my father march to and from the oats bin. To the hammer mill. To the bin. I count the seconds he has his back turned, then rush through the door and crouch behind the heavy fan mill. The sound of the hammer mill fills the granary to overflowing. I don't know what I'm hiding from. To the hammer mill. To the bin again. I scramble up the wooden ladder into the darkness and stand on the narrow plank wall separating two bins—one of barley, the other of flax. I balance myself with a firm grip on the rafters overhead. Above me, in near darkness, a metal grain spout dangles from a frayed rope, twisting in the moving air. I watch my father's stitching path to and from the oats bin, the empty pail bumping his leg. The hammer mill. The bin. Though my father is tall and thin, he looks compressed from my position, as if under a huge weight. I ball up my right hand into a fist to warm it . . . *lange Mathis . . . Dippe-Lecker . . .*

I am a gull flying north.

Below my feet, the tiny flax seeds glow up at me, their oily smell rising to my nose through the dry dust. Flax seeds are so small and slippery, a body would sink through them as through quicksand. I've heard that it has happened. Twice. No names are attached to these drownings. I can feel my thumb and index again. I am not sure what quicksand is.

That night, in a dream, I open a door and below my feet lies a huge smooth-sided cavern, rectangular in shape with rounded corners. Down low, in the half-light, endless glistening flax. By force of will I stay where I am, though I feel drawn to the edge. My foot begins to slide. I come awake, struggling. I try to calm myself. In the silence of my room, I hear a gasping sound. I think it is the wind in the tree outside my window; but it comes from my chest, as if a hole were leaking air from my lungs. I say Jesus Mary Joseph. I say Jesus Mary Joseph. I say Jesus Mary Joseph. I say Jesus . . . I dream again. My dream: I stand, my head cocked to one side, birdlike, listening.

I stare into the dark. What is accident? A man drowns in flax; a hired man shoots himself after Mass on Sunday morning; a neck-heavy bull crushes a squealing farmer whose arms flail at the massive head of the bull he had so carefully dehorned as a calf. Or this: a man falls from a haymow, a hayrope around his neck, his feet and ankles just visible to his family at the barn door. Aunt Suzanna is dead. I am afraid and I don't know why.

That afternoon, returning from school, I catch the first sound of the *Todes-glock'* from the church, ringing a death. I stop and count with Cletus the bell-ringer, one for each year. I wonder who it could be, what unforeseen danger, what unspoken illness. The tolling stops at thirty-five. It can't be. I begin to run, two steps then three when I hear the bell again and I stop. It's not for us. It's not for us. The sound fades, keeps ringing, then dies of a change in the wind.

From the road I see a car by the barn. I race across the muddy yard and through the barn door. The calf is being born; the head is out and what seems like too much neck. Its purple tongue hangs from the side of its mouth. The cow-doctor is working awkwardly around the calf's head, trying to turn its body. His hands, covered by long rubber gloves, are inside the heifer. The calf is too large to shift. The front feet and legs should be coming out at the same time as the head, but the long legs are still inside, holding the calf prisoner. The heifer's body convulses, as if being seized from within. The brown hair on her belly stands on end. She is exhausted and staggers side to side in the too-large stall. A burst of powdery dust rises from the oats straw. Deep inside my head, I feel the stab of my earache.

I go to her head. Even her eyes bulge out. I know enough not to touch her. She stares at me unseeing. She wants to lie down: her right knee is already bent. The cow doctor tells my father to keep her wedged against the side of the stall. The doctor is working fast. He hands me a nose hold to clamp into the soft sensitive parts of her nose. I try to attach the clamp, but she moves too fast. Her sticky drool flies in long arcs.

My father comes to help me. Kicking at the uneaten hay, he plants his feet in the curved concrete manger. Gently, he wedges her head against the metal stanchion with his lanky body. Annoyed, she throws him against the manger with a flick of her head. He comes back again, rubbing his hip and again, slowly forces her head to the side, his white knuckles locked around the vertical water-pipe. I insert the nose hold and she bellers in pain as it touches the inside of her nose. Together my father and I draw her head up. He tells me to snake it through the metal frame of the stanchion, snugging the rope in a double wrap around the metal pipe, exposing the soft underside of her neck. She bellers and rolls her eyes almost white. She dare not move her head. She wants to move her body away from the doctor, but cannot.

Again and again, the cow doctor tries to bring the legs up. It is hopeless. He has no choice. With one blow from a heavy mallet to the center of the forehead, the calf is dead. The doctor runs to his car and returns holding a meat saw. Grim-faced, on tiptoe, he tightens the skin with thumb and index and begins his cut. He severs the flesh and grating neckbone in a shower of blood. He calls my father to come. The calf's head and neck slump into my father's arms. Blood pours from the calf's body onto my father's legs. He cradles the calf's head awkwardly thens lowers it to the floor, his face like wood ash.

The doctor is back inside with his long rubber gloves, reaching for the legs to bring them up. The heifer moans and staggers, raising more dust. She bellers in protest. I can't breathe fast enough. Her body convulses again. She twists her head, but carefully, because of the painful clamp. I want to look away, but every particle of dust, every straw, every fiber in the rope leaps out at me. The heifer humps her back to push. A strangled sound comes from deep inside her, emptying into my ear. The tightened rope in my hand quivers as she tries to bring her head down. The nose hold prevents her and she bellers through the liquid caught in her throat. I want to cover my eyes and ears but cannot. I stare at the dim bulb enveloped in the dust that rises to form a halo of light, a circle of fire that pulsates and glows like a mock sun. It is going away from me. I see it as if beckoning me to enter into the quivering blaze. I fly into the dazzling specks of dust, each a separate world. I am taken up.

From nowhere, a warm hand covers mine. My father gently uncurls the claw my right hand has become and lowers my arm to my side. He loosens the rope, lowers the heifer's head and undoes the nose hold. She swings her head around, barely missing me. She turns to look behind her. The headless body of the dead calf lies on the bloodied concrete floor, its mutilated shape shrouded by a gray-blue film. My father stares at me, then takes my hand and leads me to the door. I look back at the young heifer. The light in her brown eyes is dim. Her head sways then sinks slowly into the manger. I stop to look, grief rising in my throat. But she raises her head again, her mouth full of hay.

My feet come to rest on a dry spot in the muddy yard. Through the fine mist, a gull clears the northwest corner of the busch. Three more gulls, then another. They come singly, in pairs, in groups of three then five, eyes sweeping the land as if looking for signposts, wing to flashing wing. I listen to the whir of feather and bone. The column moves toward the gray horizon of the southeast, a pulsing of gray and white.

My right hand tingles with warmth; a cool mist rinses the tears from my face. In this moment I resolve, should I slip, I will fall into barley.

DUKE KLASSEN is a native of Spring Hill, Minnesota, in Stearns County. He is a fifth-generation member of one of the many extended families there. At the age of thirteen, he entered the seminary, where he spent nine years studying for the Catholic priesthood. He worked as an Arabic translator during his four years in the Army Security Agency.

He received the *Chelsea* Award for Fiction and the Loft's Children's Literary Award. He was a winner in *Story*'s 1994 Short Short Story Competition and a finalist in *Best American Short Stories of 1994*. In 1995 he won first place in the California Writers' Club competition and was a finalist in *Glimmer Train*'s Award for New Writers competition. In 1996 he won a First and Second in the Green River Writers contest.

He and his wife, LaDes Glanzer, are silversmiths and live in Minneapolis, Minnesota with their three daughters Ariana, Brenna, and Ivy Klassen-Glanzer.